Summerf

Summerfolk

ESSAYS CELEBRATING SHAKESPEARE AND
THE STRATFORD THEATRES

Edited by Stanley Wells

LONG BARN BOOKS

PUBLISHED BY
LONG BARN BOOKS

Ebrington, Gloucestershire GL55 6NW

First published in 1997
1 3 5 7 9 10 8 6 4 2

Set in 11/14pt Monotype Garamond
Printed and bound by St Edmundsbury Press, Bury St Edmunds

ISBN 0 952 8285 2 9

Contents

Acknowledgements

The Editor and Publisher are grateful to the following for permission to reprint extracts:

'The Lost Gloves' by Kenneth Branagh from *Beginning* (Chatto and Windus 1989); 'The Night of *Richard III*' by Antony Sher from *Year of the King* (Methuen 1985); 'A Round of Drinks with John Barton' by Donald Sinden from *A Touch of the Memoirs* (Hodder and Stoughton, 1976).

Editor's Note

This lively collection is designed to appeal to anyone interested in Shakespeare and the theatre, although it came about to celebrate the fiftieth RSC Summer School.

I am grateful to the contributors for the enthusiasm and skill they have brought to the enterprise and for meeting tight deadlines. Paul Edmondson supplied invaluable research assistance. Mrs Etta Mahon and Kelly Costigan generously helped in keyboarding the entries. My wife, Susan Hill, not only publishes the book but has been an indefatigable collaborator at every stage.

Foreword

ADRIAN NOBLE

I was part of a generation which was intoxicated by Stratford. As soon as University term finished and we had earned some cash working on the local motorway extension, we would hitch-hike north up the A38 to Stratford and camp for several weeks, courtesy of many anonymous local farmers. We would stand at the back of the Royal Shakespeare Theatre or sit in the gallery, queue for returns at The Other Place, seeing every show as many times as possible, ferociously debating the productions, hanging around the stage door, drinking deep of this magical, heady atmosphere that is Stratford in summertime.

If I spent much of my youth peering over the garden wall so to speak, I've spent most of my working life with my head down, tending the garden, or presently, as head gardener.

This charming book offers a welcome opportunity to look around and look back over 50 years.

The RSC Summer School, whose golden jubilee this book celebrates, reflects many of the values that are fundamental to our artistic family. It is devoted to Shakespeare in a knowledgeable and open-minded way; it is scholarly, but not fusty or school-masterly; it can be serious but never solemn; it likes a bit of ritual and pattern, and most of all it is fun. It has had very few long-serving, hard-working directors: first John Garrett, a Bristol headmaster; John Wilders taking over in 1960, followed by Stanley Wells in 1971, who was joined by Robert Smallwood as co-director in 1992. Over the years the School has become a much-loved highlight of the Stratford summer scene, and under Stanley's directorship, involvement of actors and directors has greatly increased, furthering the interaction between the academic and the theatrical worlds.

Our Stratford is a unique community of artists, artisans, administrators, technicians, academics, writers, passionate devotees, passing visitors, all of whom are drawn to the extraordinary energy that comes from the nexus of birthplace, stage and last resting place. These essays are a wonderful kaleidoscope of memories, some funny, some sentimental, many full of insight into the workings of that community. The characters are vivid, the stories are well-told, evocative and amusing, and through the pages the personality of a very special time and place emerges.

THE ACTORS

Stratford upon Haven

JANE LAPOTAIRE

To play Shakespeare AND live in the country? Bliss. 'What girl could ask for more?' I said jokingly as a defence against being thought too eager and enthusiastic about joining the RSC – cynicism was de rigueur in the 70's, but I was seriously overjoyed at the thought. That thought, twenty-three years old now, has been weathered and re-shaped since when, in 1974, I first played Viola in *Twelfth Night* for Peter Gill; Lady Macduff (and other parts too embarrassing to mention) in Trevor Nunn's production of *Macbeth*; and Sonja in *Uncle Vanya*, played and directed by Nicol Williamson. But apart from a few nips and tucks in my attitude to tourist-filled streets when I'm pressed for time shopping for Sunday lunch before a Saturday matinée, not much has changed in the surge of pleasure I feel when I say I'm in the RSC at Stratford for a season. But the reasons for that delight are now manifold. They, and I, have changed with 'the inaudible and noiseless foot of time'.

There is a bonding that takes place amongst actors left to their own devices and the sole companionship of their colleagues at the end of the M40, that is particular and special to this place. The company grows very close without the distractions or dispersal of the London effect, actors falling out of their rented homes on Waterside a few seconds before the half is called, instead of having to trek into The Barbican from the wilds of Kensal Rise despite the vagaries of the Northern line or arriving jaded by the traffic jams in Lewisham. I can make it into the theatre in twelve minutes from my rented cottage in Ilmington if I put my foot down. A drive largely through country lanes seasonally edged with hoar frost, or the first brave green spears of snowdrops, or heavy-eared waves of wheat. The journey from my home in Putney – the same distance of some eight miles or so, from SW15 to EC2 – takes me the best part of a nerve-frazzling hour. The majority of the company – apart from the young mums with young children learning how to juggle acting, mothering and housekeeping in a new home – are freed from the intrusive albeit endearing demands of a family, and have the luxury of being able to concentrate solely on The Work.

The play's the thing. Or the voice classes – individual tuition, or company warm-ups before each show. Or John Barton's sonnet classes, reacted to prior to the event with some groaning or occasional mutters of 'School' and referred to after with astonishment, gratitude and pleasure. John can untangle the trickiest of texts, the densest of imagery with such ease and naturalness that even the most terrified of actors coming to the Bard for the first time feel empowered to do their own decoding and demystifying after a class with John. A season at Stratford is now the longest contractual opportunity available to actors to work on classical texts. Even at the National Theatre actors are employed play by play. There are eleven months of work on a Stratford season – including early rehearsals which often take place initially in London – and then a further two months in Newcastle and Plymouth before a possible run of another four months or so at The Barbican.

It is vitally important for young actors to have a sense of continuity in their professional development. Vitally important, too, that barriers and defences are removed so that the actor is in touch with his centre, and from this centre is able to grow. There is skill and support available for this at every hand. It is not every actor's choice, of course, this continuation of the learning process begun at drama school. But for those of us who want more than a ten day shoot on a television programme, four days on a radio play or a couple of days on a feature film, where there is neither the inclination nor the possibility of lowering defences amongst strangers for so short a period, or the time or facility for learning, it is a heaven-sent opportunity to push professional horizons back and to grow. And it's free. Eleven months with some of the greatest texts in the English language, and the greatest classical texts in any language. We live on words. The actual bread and butter of living is a different matter. Keeping a home on in London is a luxury and a struggle. Double electricity, gas, and telephone bills. The pay isn't up to television levels, but the work is soul food. We love words.

After all this edification we can then fall out of the theatre into the Dirty Duck for legalised drinking after hours. An arrangement solely and specially for the actors. Special. That's what this place makes you feel. Even the lowliest of Company Members straight out of drama school stand a chance of being recognised, and having their work appreciated by passers-by in the streets, especially if they happen to be outspoken and open hearted American students, and especially if they, the LCMs, happen to look shapely in a doublet and hose. Little groups of autograph hunters huddle round the stage door after a performance in the hope of chatting to the actors. Or if Ken Branagh's in the show you can expect a healthy group of Branagh groupies giggling and jostling in their dozens. Most of us are blessed with one avid fan. I have an inexplicable following of gay guys and a curious collection of middle-aged women, who I suspect either want to mother me or give me a square meal. One woman respectably dressed and quite shy said modestly to me one night, 'I laughed and I cried, I can't say more than that.' No indeed ma'am. That was special. I've never forgotten it. It's special too to be playing Shakespeare in his home town. Audiences are drawn here from all over the world, – for the acting and the production, – there's a little you can do about the former but precious little about the latter. Multi-national audiences are not always a blessing for performers either, when line after comedy line is met with a crashing silence resounding from the auditorium. 'What's wrong with me tonight?' said Mary Rutherford to me in the wings after one of her entrances as Olivia, 'not a single laugh.' 'Hang on,' I said trying to be comforting. 'I'm long sighted. I'll give them the once over. Maybe we're all off tonight.' We talk like that backstage, when we're not chatting in iambic pentameters, of course. What 'they' are like is always the main consideration in the wings during a performance. After my next entrance I said 'Wall-to-wall Japanese, all smiling politely and enjoying it immensely, but uttering nary a sound.'

Of course there are days when you feel that the performance is on a tourist itinerary; yesterday Canterbury Cathedral, tomorrow the Lake District, today, the theatre; and that a visit to see a Shakespeare play in Shakespeare's home town is more an obligatory notch on a tourist trophy than a real pleasure, but those occasions are rare.

At the opposite end of this scale are the Shakespeare buffs, the Academics at the Shakespeare Centre and the Institute, bowers of intellectual stimulus – especially the Institute with its exquisite garden – and sometimes places of acute nervous tension for actors faced with an inquiring audience at a question-and-answer session after a specific production in which they are appearing. Members of the public from every walk of life, who are drawn to the various Shakespeare courses and summer schools, have often made a lifelong study of the entire canon and their knowledge and percipience can be quite daunting, when an average acting career spanning some thirty years may give the actor only a working knowledge of some fifteen or so of the thirty-seven plays. But it's frequently a fruitful exchange. The actor departs gratefully with a small fee, and a more specific understanding of what has been understood and appreciated, or misunderstood in both senses, in the production, and the audience have had a chance to taste what it's like to be up there on the stage doing it and not simply reading it or watching it.

The still small centre in this learning world is for me Holy Trinity Church. Here He is buried. Or at least He is reputed to be. Almost all aspects of Shakespeare's life and work are disputed, and his last resting place is not exempt from the continuing debate. Perhaps the fat burghers of Stratford knew they were on to a good thing even then in 1616. It certainly seems questionable, even given the small amount of fame that he had accrued in his lifetime, that what amounted to a middle-class family should be buried in the chancel of a church. That was a last resting place usually reserved for the nobility of rank, not of literature. And the flagstone with his name on it and its rather admonitory poem as a warning to body snatchers, seems to indicate a person of exceptionally small proportions, unless, as the common parlance goes – He was buried standing up. However, little of this matters when the failing day's light bathes the waters of the Avon and the branches of the over-hanging willows dapple the lapping waves and the backs of the many swans that flock there. A time when all but the most ardent of tourists have departed with their ashtrays stamped with that famous picture of His head, and their oven gloves replete with pictorial evidence of Anne Hathaway's cottage, it's then easy to turn one's back on the chatter and the clatter of supper in the canteen that overlooks one of the most beautiful views of the river, as do the leading actors' dressing rooms with their little balconies that give out on to it. And it's difficult to resist the lure of walking quietly through the gardens in the gathering dusk up to the church, stealing a sprig of rosemary on the way, to pay silent and grateful homage at the altar rail that guards his grave.

It's rare that a walk like this, or any through Stratford, won't bring you face to face with a local shopkeeper with time to chat – a luxury lost in the turmoil that's London – who will smile and say how pleased they are to see you back, or with the more familiar face of someone who works at the theatre. Usherettes, front-of-house staff, stage crew – we're all in it together. Boot-makers, swordmakers, dressmakers, all those people that the actor meets in the frantic costume fittings prior to an opening night in the little warren of rooms across the road from the stage door, are mostly local, and as such take enormous pride in their theatre and their work. Nothing is too much trouble.

I've known dressers hoof it up three flights of stairs minutes before an actor's entrance to retrieve a forgotten prop, a hand-kerchief, a mislaid rosary, and be back down in the wings as fast as the forty-two stone steps backstage to the top floor of dress-ing rooms of the Swan Theatre will allow.

The Swan! Whole eulogies have been written, and rightly so, about this beautiful theatre. Suffice it for me to say I don't know an actor in England who has played in it and not loved its brick and wood warmth, and the vibrancy of its relationship of stage to stalls, or an actor who hasn't played it who isn't envi-ous of those of us who have. I remember it originally as the rather sombre and musty conference room where we would rehearse. Not a sad loss, especially as the building of the Swan gives us actors now an exquisite rehearsal space on the top floor, again all golden wood, with a panorama of the rooftops of the town and a spectacular birdseye view of the river, – safe from the smell that rain often churns up from the river bed, – a room named after one of the most loved and innately gra-cious of all great actors, Peggy Ashcroft.

That's another thing about playing great classical roles at Stratford. There is an element of stepping into other people's shoes. That can be quite daunting. Taking on the mantle from names that were heroes in one's theatre-besotted youth. 'Best not read the reviews' advised Peter Gill – wisely as it turned out – just prior to my first first night in *Twelfth Night*. 'They'll only compare your Viola to Dorothy Tutin's/Vanessa Red-grave's/etc.etc., best not to know.' It was advice I heeded. I haven't read a review from that day to this until long after the production is over. Then it's just so much fish-and-chip paper, or a question of 'Death, where is thy sting?' Any actor that says he isn't affected by bad reviews isn't being honest, and the good

9

ones may isolate certain moments for praise that are then dead to you for ever.

Shakespeare's birth and death are celebrated on the same day when the town is closed to traffic and literally hundreds of people walk through the streets, through the Birthplace laden with posies and garlands of flowers, and bedecked with buttonholes or sprigs of rosemary 'for remembrance' tied with yellow and purple ribbons and, one by one, the bouquets are laid in tribute on his grave. It's a great honour to be asked to walk in this procession as a member of the RSC and hard not to be affected by the excitement and the general air of festivity that commingles finally in the huge marquee after the service in his memory in the church, at which actors and musicians from the RSC take part, the huge and tepid tent bursting with sweltering dignitaries from all over the world, be-chained and be-furred mayors from local boroughs, churchmen and Members of Parliament all replete with the importance of their office and a large and lavish lunch.

It's a day that makes me proud to be in the theatre. No easy feat, given the bad press and the belittling 'luvviedom' label that the tabloids seem to delight in giving the profession – a term never used by any of us in the business. But this is not a day for carping. It is a day for being proud to be an actor. A day for remembering that the greatest playwright who ever lived also trod the boards.

Many actors, avid walkers like myself and country lovers, once seduced by the beauty of the neighbouring Cotswold hills and their exquisite villages of thatched rooves and Tudor beams often make their permanent homes here. It's a dream I've had for most of the twenty-three years that I've been in and out of the RSC. But there's a disquieting rumour that once you move here, chances are that you never work for the company again. So for the moment it must stay a dream and I'll stay put, and take out that season ticket on the M40, and still feel that surge of pleasure when I see the theatre as I round the Clopton Bridge.

My University

RICHARD PASCO

I had for some time wanted to visit the theatre in Stratford, but the rigours of life led me in every direction BUT Warwickshire. I had worked as an apprentice-assistant-stage-manager (the lowest form of animal life in the theatre) at the Old Q Theatre in London, having been told that my efforts at school would never get me through the School Certificate let alone to Oxford or Cambridge to read English Literature, which in later years I longed to do (and still do!). Fate directed me into HM Forces in 1944 and I was imprisoned in khaki for three and a half years. Opportunities presented themselves to act in Army entertainments but I was still convinced that I wanted to be a producer – as directors were termed in my youth – or even, God help me, a Film Director! In January 1948 on demobilisation I was given a place at the Central School of Speech and Drama, as my budding career in the theatre had been curtailed by Serving my King and Country and the Government of the day made grants to ex-servicemen to resume their studies. Two years at Central taught me a great deal. Most important perhaps was my voice work with Gwynneth Thurburn, who taught me such profundities as how to breathe from and use the diaphragm – essential when performing one of the great Shakespearian roles – (the way that many of today's actors heave from the chest annoys me) but technique of mind and body was essential teaching from my beloved teachers at Central. Apart from Thurbie another profound influence at Drama School was a later stalwart of the Stratford theatre company, Raymond Westwell, who taught us how to think within the framework of play and character. Such simplicities as 'where have you come from' and 'where are you going' in this scene, were simple objectives and a great deal more besides. Perhaps inklings of the 'Stanislavski Method' seeped into Raymond's teaching methods.

During this two-year 'Refresher Course', in the holidays fellow students took themselves off to work in cafés or hotels to earn money to augment the grant's sparse allowance for day-to-day living. Fees were generously paid, but there was not much petty cash for life outside the school. So in the long summer break of 1949 a group of some dozen or so students from my year took ourselves off to Whitby, Yorkshire, to do a six-week season of plays in the form of 'Weekly Rep'. We were given an empty church hall, with tiny stage and limited lighting, and we did everything – painted the sets, rehearsed the plays, sold the tickets, and put up posters around the town, where allowed, to try to sell our wares to an untried public. We were rewarded with packed houses – some three hundred odd people per evening and about half that number at Wednesday and Saturday matinées. Our programme consisted of popular plays of the time – we did not attempt Shakespeare – such as *Blithe Spirit*, *Grand National*

Night, *Our Town*, *Berkeley Square*, *Fools Rush In*, and so on.

At the end of my course I found myself – at long last – coming to Stratford on the train to stand at the back of the stalls to watch Tyrone Guthrie's production of *King Henry VIII* with Anthony Quayle as the King, Andrew Cruickshank as Wolsey and Gwen Ffrangçon-Davies as Queen Katharine. I was simply staggered by the fact that as one entered the auditorium there was no curtain or act-drop visible – there was the set in front of the audience ready to be presently occupied by the actors as the house-lights dimmed and the 'two hours traffic' commenced. It was an exciting innovation which I had never seen in the theatre before and which we now all take for granted – perhaps unfortunately because I know a number of theatregoers miss so much of the illusory magic of the theatre with the curtain going up and the impedimenta of lighting gantries etc. discreetly hidden behind what I knew in my stage management days as a 'Tormentor.' Perhaps a young director will appear shortly and re-discover 'The Curtain' and receive an award for so doing ...

I did not visit the Stratford theatre again for a few years, as my own career began to shape itself. In the early 1950s there was no overnight success in the shape of star roles in the major companies. Young actors and actresses expected, at best, after Drama School or University to get into a good repertory company and then perhaps join the major companies as a walk-on or spear-carrier. There was very little television so the opportunity to go from a leading role on the small screen into playing the major classical roles at Stratford or the Old Vic hardly existed. Anyway, the required techniques to handle, say, *Hamlet* or *Henry V* had not been learnt – the voice will not carry very far after an hour, let alone three and a half hours followed by a hectic sword-fight, unless the ground is prepared first. There is a great deal to be learned by watching one's peers in the theatre and this I began to do when offered a contract at the Old Vic to 'play as cast and understudy as required' for two years in a company comprising Peggy Ashcroft, Donald Wolfit, Alec Clunes, Roger Livesey, Ursula Jeans, Robert Eddison, Leo McKern, Paul Rogers and directors of the calibre of Tyrone Guthrie, Glen Byam Shaw, Michel St. Denis, Hugh Hunt, Hilton Edwards and many others; and so, almost unconsciously I realise, began the long haul towards the goal of playing the great roles at Stratford.

I subsequently worked at the Birmingham Rep. for three years, at the Royal Court Theatre for the English Stage Company for a further period of years and again, having failed an audition with Peter Hall for the RSC's Quatercentenary *Wars of the Roses* season, I presented a modest performance of *Henry V* and Berowne in *Love's Labour's Lost* for the Bristol Old Vic in Bristol and for nine months all over Europe and Israel.

People interested enough in my career can follow my progress in other theatre reference books – but the point I wish to make is that through all these years of working, watching and performing, the rehearsal and preparatory period was essentially of short duration. In Birmingham there was the luxury of three weeks rehearsal and four weeks playing (rehearsing all day and performing in the evening that is). At the Royal Court we had perhaps three to four weeks rehearsal, and at Bristol there was one hectic period when I was performing Peer Gynt in the evenings and all day rehearsing Jack Tanner in Shaw's *Man and Superman*. This exhausted me, because the only time to learn Shaw's complex text was at night after a performance and a hurried supper. I never experienced a long period in weekly rep or, indeed, twice nightly – twice weekly, – the mind boggles! The order of the day was learn the lines and the moves, make sure your flies are buttoned, and don't bump into the furniture.

An account of how I eventually got into the RSC is too long and boring to relate here, but I did a workout (a lengthy exploratory audition) for Trevor Nunn and Terry Hands and John Barton and was accepted for the 1969 season. My parts were Polixenes in *The Winter's Tale*, Buckingham in *Henry VIII*, Leantio in *Women Beware Women* and Valentine in the Theatre-go-round production of *The Two Gentlemen of Verona*. After twenty-five odd years of very mixed experience in theatre of all kinds I was about to enter my University, finally and gratefully. There was anything between seven and ten weeks rehearsal for each production and all the elements that lay in my actor's brain and bank of instincts were to be tried and tested and brought into play. Voice work, movement, study of Shakespearian language and countless other instruments were to be tuned and played upon. All that I had missed in not going to university, being kicked out of school, serving in the army, and the years in other theatres, were now to be eclipsed by the good fortune of activity in Stratford. I was not only being directed by fine directors but all around me were my Cambridge scholars: John Barton who guided me – in every sense of the word – through *Twelfth Night* and most especially in *Richard II* in which Ian Richardson and I alternated the parts of the King and Bolingbroke; Stanley Wells who became a friend outside the theatre and provided patient help and the fluency of his edition of the text of *Richard II* which we used as our working version; and also by introduction to the legendary George 'Dadie' Rylands who gave me exacting work and scholarly aid in recordings for the Argo

Record Company of Shakespeare's plays. Peter Orr – himself a pupil of Dadie's at Cambridge and then the 'Spoken Word' director of Argo Records – asked me to record the Sonnets of Shakespeare and to make many other recordings of poetry – Hardy, Gerard Manley Hopkins, and many more.

Likewise I formed a rewarding and, I hope, lifelong friendship with Roger and Marian Pringle, now Director and Chief Librarian respectively of the Shakespeare Birthplace Trust, who were always on hand to help me with access to the phenomenal archives of the Trust.

The rehearsal process in those years at Stratford – 1969–74, and later 1979–82 – was a revelation. Exploration of all facets of the characters we were called upon to portray – the backgrounds of their lives, their emotional, intellectual and sexual whims and ambiguities were delved into and expressed through the ever-relevant and profound texts we were holding in our hands. The ways that an actor can convey the most subtle and involved meanings of Shakespeare's text to the ears of a modern audience were exhausted and were always pertinent even to the news of the day, starkly present in the newspaper headlines, on television news etc. 'Shakespeare Lives' etc. etc.

The seasons passed by and in retrospect I cannot really believe that I was able to respond to all the stimuli presented to me, so that the development of the intellect kept pace with the instinct which I worked upon as an actor and I could now, quite often, be ahead of the director.

In one season I was asked if I would like to play Jaques in *As You Like It*. Thinking myself too young and unsuited by temperament to the part I asked to be excused, but was persuaded by Trevor Nunn to at least meet and talk with Buzz Goodbody (the late and much lamented director who had been John

Barton's assistant when I first arrived in Stratford in 1969 and who had patiently helped me learn the seemingly impossible text of Thomas Middleton's *Women Beware Women*) who was being given her first Main House production with *As You Like It*. Buzz persuaded me to play the part quite simply. We had supper together and at the coffee stage she produced a postcard reproduction of Joseph Severn's drawing of John Keats, saying that 'this was Jaques as a young man,' and after a pause produced from her capacious handbag a reproduction of Graham Sutherland's portrait of Somerset Maugham, saying 'and this is Jaques at the time of the play'. I was completely won over by this talented and extraordinary young director and accepted her offer on the spot, such was the process of being able, by simple example, to know what might be the end result of a study of character. I loved playing Jaques and can modestly say that it was one of my most successful performances – acting in Stratford.

Our work with John Barton on the now legendary production of *Richard II* with two actors alternating the roles of the King and Bolingbroke would almost occupy a volume in itself, but perhaps a few words will illustrate the working process of the Company which I was now accustomed to and willingly embraced. The daily 'calls' pinned on the notice board for the following day's rehearsal would often simply say '10.30 – Mr. Pasco, Solus.' This meant that I had perhaps an hour of work on the text on my own with John. I referred to them as my 'tutorials.' Rhythm, metre, light and shade, rallentando, diminuendo were all part and parcel of the study. Deciding how far to suggest, in the early stages of the play, Richard's true personality under the kingly exterior, John's direction to me was to 'show-off – the actor in love with the role of playing the King.'

Benson played him as a 'luxurious lounger caressing and feeding his hounds in bored indifference.' John Gielgud (a notable *Richard II* in the 1930s) has written that the actor must use the early scenes to create an impression of slyness and petty vanity and callous indifference, and of course the more one sets this up the more moving is the later downfall. He reveals both scorn and fear of Bolingbroke, but his positive belief in the divine right of kings gives him the security of his hereditary kingship.

> Not all the water in the rough rude sea
> Can wash the balm off from an anointed King,
> The breath of worldly men cannot depose
> The deputy elected by the Lord.

He later launches into the first of his great solo speeches, a meditation on mortality which gives classic expression to the theme of the vanity of human greatness. Richard is beginning to learn that the facade of kingship may offer inadequate shelter to the human being who dwells behind it. The rest of this great play is doubtless familiar to lovers of Shakespeare, and perhaps what I have just written gives some idea of the thoroughness and complexity of the rehearsal process adopted by the RSC and its eminent directors. After all the years working in the ordinary fashion of the theatre – 'get the play on at all costs' in three or four weeks – these weeks of study and concentration were the culmination of hopes and indeed dreams. And so it was for me, through the plays I have mentioned and *Murder in the Cathedral* – T. S. Eliot's powerful drama of Thomas À Becket – *The Lower Depths*, Gorky's study of human degradation, *Man and Superman* by Bernard Shaw, and many others. And in the old Other Place was a production of *Timon of Athens* in a studio theatre ambience. This was an altogether different process in rehearsal and presentation, a cast of only fourteen or so actors and a limited area both technically and in performance to fill. The director was Ron Daniels and we had the good fortune to be able to turn to the late Professor Philip Brockbank for excellent textual and scholastic help. It was his favourite play and we duly wanted to do it justice. The play has been described by various critics over the years as 'unsatisfactory,' 'unwieldy,' 'unfinished', and so on and on ... But for me, working on and playing the part over a season, I realised it is a grossly neglected masterpiece, which explores dramatically man's inhumanity to man and the outward manifestations of the human psyche under stress. It deals with disillusionment, despair and grief, all of which produce a total weariness of body and spirit – an extremely rewarding epic-character for any actor to come to terms with – and a discipline imposed on him by the physical limits of The Other Place and the close proximity of the audience.

Working in the old Other Place was so rewarding – that almost mystical experience between actor and audience which can produce pin-dropping silence and concentration (if it is not interrupted by coughing, fidgeting, programme fanning and now the ever-present hum of the air-conditioning plant) was all to the fore because there were none of the latter distractions available! It was virtually a corrugated iron-roofed shed, stiflingly hot in summer and pretty cold in winter, but the proximity of player to audience was quite unique and another facet of acting in Stratford which I embraced willingly.

So much has changed in the interim. But I will not forget the moments of contemplation when walking out onto the dressing-room balcony at different times of day, to watch the slow passing of the year and the inner peace that came as a reward to being fortunate enough to be a player in the leading Shakespearian company in the world: perhaps, reluctantly, preparing for a matinée of *Richard II* with the curtains drawn and the windows closed to keep out the noise of people enjoying themselves in boats on the river outside on a boiling hot summer's afternoon; the peace of twilight and the oncoming night looking up the river towards Holy Trinity Church in moonlight, before going down to the stage to 'take the call' and the reward of vociferous applause from the audience, and as one ascended the stairs to take off the garb of king or clown and the greasepaint, to the thoughts of, 'Do I really deserve it? Have I given of my best?' In the culmination of circumstances – I hope so.

A Pause for Breath

PHILIP VOSS

As a Leicester lad, my visits to the almost local memorial Theatre in Stratford-upon-Avon gave me my first taste of big-time theatre. Laurence Harvey leaping from the Motley set as Romeo and landing with thin and shaky legs. Olivier as *Macbeth* with heavy make-up and huge knees. Vivien Leigh, imagining the perfumes of Arabia on slender wrists. Later on, Laughton as Bottom and Lear. Theatrical glamour at its height. Then in 1960 I got there. A telegram from Peter Hall, no less. 'We need you. Start February 9th.' My ambition come to fruit at eleven pounds ten shillings a week.

There was a cocktail party in the circle bar. Hot off the Midland Red bus, I entered to see Peggy Ashcroft running across the room to say 'Darling, how are you?' to Dorothy Tutin. Hester Collyer herself and Hedwig in the same room. I never fully recovered from star-shock for the rest of the season. Peter O'Toole who, at twenty six, was about to give his matchless performance of Shylock with myself playing the definitive and blacked-up Nubian Slave. 'Blacking up!' That wouldn't happen now. An actor called Ian Richardson was at the party. He was playing The Lord in *The Taming of the Shrew* I discovered. (Oh the security of that definite article). Soon he would astound everyone with his hilariously decrepit and ancient Aragon and later by his pathetic Sir Andrew Aguecheek. He became a star within the season. In *The Winter's Tale*, I was 'A Lord'. I had flicked through the script and saw there was indeed something called 'The First Lord' and 'The Second Lord' and 'The Third Lord'; all of which were quite tasty, but when it came to it, my 'A Lord' had just over half a line – 'What fit is this, good lady?' – some way into Paulina's long tirade against Leontes. How do you say it? How do you stress it? While Ashcroft was tearing her lace, I slipped in my small contribution as discreetly as possible. It's taken me years to realise that Shakespeare probably only put in the line to give Paulina a chance to snatch a huge breath for the rest of her onslaught.

In Peter Hall's revival of his own production of *Twelfth Night*, I carried on a bay tree in a tub for the gulling scene. The ravishing sets were by Lila de Nobili, including gauze back-cloths, which she painted herself with a yard broom. When lit, it seemed as though shafts of sunlight were streaming through them. If I came into the wings early enough I could catch Tutin in her first scene with Olivia.

> Make me a willow cabin at your gate,
> And call upon my soul within the house;
> Write loyal cantons of contemnèd love
> And sing them loud even in the dead of night;
> Halloo your name to the reverberate hills
> And make the babbling gossip of the air
> Cry out 'Olivia!'

It was incredible. I had never realised that verse speaking could be so thrilling. The babbling gossip of the air did indeed reverberate when she hallooed 'Olivia'. How did she do it? We were to learn.

On alternate Saturday mornings, John Barton, guru extraordinary, the guiding influence behind Shakespearian verse speaking at the RSC for the past thirty years or so, would show us how it was done. Scansion. Anti-scansion. Count and counterpoint. Irony. Antithesis. Structure and the caesura: the blasted caesura. Do you breathe on it? Do you pause on it? Or do you bounce off it and run on? Using the sonnets, as the perfect form in miniature of the whole, he would instruct, inform, and then analyse our efforts. It was torture. To stand in front of a class and launch into 'That time of year thou mayest in me behold . . .' when the only thing to behold was the utter fear and to finish knowing he was going to say 'Very good. Now what was wrong with that?' was character building to say the least. It meant a lot of tears on the Midland Red bus. But! What he gave me! It was an influence on my acting and speaking that I have never forgotten, I couldn't, and for which I shall always be grateful.

On the other Saturday mornings, he taught us how to fight. It was an intriguing system whereby all the showy energy went on the outward preparation, so as to catch the audience's eye, while the actual stroke on your opponent was relatively light. I am sure it was very good. In any event, it was to prepare us for the forthcoming production of *Troilus and Cressida*.

Dorothy Tutin again and Denholm Elliot in his last juvenile role. He felt too old for the part and self-denigratingly told us that he had tits like spaniels' ears and was unhappy. He was thirty-seven. Max Adrian, unforgettable as Pandarus. 'Peter, I can't play it like this. I have to imagine the warriors at the back of the stalls. If the audience actually see them coming up from below the stage – there is no army, it's too slow and my eyes are always down.' 'Well, show me what you mean.' So he did. As if auditioning he demonstrated the way he wanted to play the scene where all the Trojan heroes return from the war. 'You're right,' said Peter Hall, 'We'll do it that way.' An actor in conflict with a director! And winning. I've done that since – and it costs.

Derek Godfrey, a very noble Hector – Patrick Allen, Achilles with a young Dinsdale Landen, a witty and grinning Patroclus. We played in a sandpit designed by Leslie Hurry, set against a deep red cyclorama, embossed by a mapping pen in black ink. I knew it well. Or at least, one square yard of it. I was a Greek Guard in fibreglass armour with helmet, standing with my back to the audience for the Council scene (Twenty-five minutes) and Achilles' attempted entrapment (Twenty minutes). My arms were outstretched throughout and in each hand – a spear. We need you? For what? Scenery!

Eric Porter played Ulysses. I was his understudy, so although I rarely saw his performance, I heard it many, many times. He was a troubled man, friendly enough, but distant, and his acting had a glacial and precise quality about it. His body was squeezed almost into the shape of the letter 'C' when he played Leontes, as he tried hard to release the emotion needed for those destructive, jealous rages. For Ulysses, though, he was perfect. He had very long, expressive fingers and would prod the air with them as he made each point in the degree and time speeches. He had authority, indisputable intelligence and was upright. The production was a landmark and passionately remembered by all who saw it. The sand became a symbol – running through Tutin's fingers – after she'd trawled her fingers through it – time running out. Paul Hardwick as Ajax building sandcastles and smashing them – the buffoon. Hector's corpse, scoring the sand in blood as he was dragged away after his Myrmidon murder.

We, the newcomers, the walk-ons, the spear-carriers, were put together in the 'L-shaped' dressing room 14, now the wig room. The silly fun we had in there! Iris Warren, legendary voice teacher of the time, gave her lessons in that room. Lying on the floor and panting to the sound of small 'f's, she would lean over us to feel our vibrant diaphragms and urge us to get in touch with our 'pips' and if we opened our eyes, we could see her fulsome pink bloomers. It was so naughty. She, of course, being intent on her work, was quite oblivious to the fact – perhaps not – but she must have wondered at the suppressed and gurgled giggles all over the room. We were young! She still, however, instilled into me techniques that I use to this day ... small 'f's and all.

At the end of the season, we went to London and became Royal. We became the Royal Shakespeare Company at the Aldwych Theatre, and opened with *The Duchess of Malfi*, which starred Peggy Ashcroft and was directed by Donald McWinnie. *Ondine* followed with Leslie Caron. We went to the first night party at the Waldorf Hotel and she wore a tiara (smallish) and a cream gown with a train. I'd given up the Midland Red bus by then and took the occasional taxi, but even so I was impressed. The fairy off the Christmas tree – and she asked me to dance! Once. John Whiting's *The Devils* followed, directed by Peter Wood, which made stars of Roy Dotrice and Diana Rigg. *Becket* by Jean Anouilh came next, with Eric Porter and Christopher Plummer, which transferred to the Globe Theatre for a six-month run and after that I was left to face the wilderness and the realities of an actor's life, without the protection of the RSC. It was thirty years before I returned. I vowed never to go back unless the parts were interesting enough to play, but, in any case, my resolve was never challenged. Then, in the late eighties, I got an offer. It didn't excite me enough, but it whetted my appetite, and I knew then that a return was on the cards. Finally, in 1990, Adrian Noble's first year as artistic director, the offer was exciting enough. To be on stage as the Lord Chief Justice and Worcester with Robert Stephens' Falstaff and to play Sir Epicure Mammon in Sam Mendes' production of '*The Alchemist*'.

The two *Henry Four* plays were rehearsed in the building the RSC owns in Clapham, so we arrived in Stratford a fairly integrated group. Cocktail parties had been modified to glasses of wine on trestle tables and if there were any 'hello darlings', they didn't stop my heart. We did have, though, Robert Stephens. He had stunned us all in the very first run-through of Part One, when wearing a red, polka-dotted headscarf, just for flavour, he took flight. He was astounding. Probably never as good again. For those of us present it will always be one of the great moments in our theatrical memory. There were gasps of admiration from us all.

We became friendly, and he was always generous to work with. Be benign, he suggested to me as the Lord Chief Justice, to start with – it gives you a longer journey. And so, we would sit at a café table for our first scene together and laugh and be good-humoured and I loved it. It was iconoclastic I'm told and of that I'm proud. He was a great kisser, Robert. The friendlier one became the more kisses one received. Big, wet, affectionate kisses, full on the mouth. A bit disgusting but then that was Robert. He loved life and I never heard him complain about his health. 'How are you, Robert?' (When his arm was inexplicably grazed or he was looking jaundiced). 'Fine, dear boy' would come the booming answer. 'Fine'!

Although 'Summer in Stratford' was much the same in feel, the mulberry tree had been hacked down and the elegant 'Mulberry Tree' restaurant, where I had eaten those devilled mushrooms, had been demolished, along with the white, wrought iron railings that fronted its verandahs. The Midland Red bus station had gone, but then, what did it matter – we all drove cars. There wasn't a cinema any more. And that did matter. Now it's a drive to the multi-complex up the M42.

In place of the Mulberry Tree there was a shopping mall of very questionable appeal. There are car parks and hotels, but all, thankfully, low-rise, so that the thirties prow-like shape of the theatre still raises excited and hopeful expectations as you approach the town.

My first few days back on that stage were uneasy. All those powerful ghosts got in the way.

The theatre itself had changed quite a lot. An apron stage jutted out beyond the old proscenium arch and the Conference Hall, where we used to rehearse the plays, had gone entirely. In its place, the glorious Swan Theatre, and above it a new rehearsal room of such beauty that one never enters it without a sense of wonder. The views across the meadows and Stratford Old Town and ahead is Holy Trinity. Whenever you look out of the window, it is there to see – the spire. The spire may not have been there when Shakespeare was around, but the church was, he's in it, we hope, so long as no-one has disturbed his bones and it must look very much the same now as when he walked about the town.

John Barton was no longer there in a permanent capacity. The following and subsequent years he gave occasional Masterclasses, but the rules had been blurred. Indeed, they were no longer called 'rules'. It was a personal choice, a feeling for the Language; still basically the same, but far less rigid. I still had my type-written pages from 1960. They are faded and yellow-ish, but I stand by them.

During my lengthy absence, I had discovered, somewhat late in my career, Stanislavski or some Anglo-American version of it. *An Actor Prepares* had rather bewildered me at RADA, but through work with Mike Alfreds at Shared Experience, I had been introduced to a way of preparation that changed my approach to acting for ever. Super-objectives, scene-objectives, actions, obstacles against them and units. I learned how to analyse a text and how to extract the author's intention for each character.

It is argued that Shakespeare doesn't require this search for the sub-text; his intentions are always stated, but, following all the rules I learned from John Barton, and adding all the ingre-dients discovered by this new analysis, I can propel the most formal speech always knowing what I want to achieve. The lan-guage becomes not only poetical, but dramatic and has an active life.

On top of this very systematic approach, there is an exercise, which can only be applied when the lines are well-learnt and the intentions are clear: 'Points of Concentration'. It puts the character through a sieve of different emotions or conditions while still maintaining the main objective of the scene. To take a simple example – temperature – heat or cold will affect the playing of a scene in different ways, so I might, while begging to save my life, examine the possibility of extreme heat on my behaviour. It can sometimes, however, lead to difficulties with other actors or the director, who may have no idea what I'm playing at. 'What's the matter with you today?' Steven Pimlott once asked me, and Denys Hawthorne was somewhat bemused when he thought I intended to play Worcester as Victor Sylvester, dogging Hotspur's every footstep one day in an attempt to establish the dominating nature of my relationship over him. In fairness, Adrian Noble, who was directing the play, never said a word, but then, he was trained at the Drama Centre, so perhaps knew what I was up to.

Coriolanus in my following season gave me the chance to use a combination of most of these techniques. Directed by David Thacker, I played Menenius, the uncle-cum-father figure to the hero, played by Toby Stephens. This was our third go. I'd played his father in the two plays prior to this production and now had an even closer relationship as his obsessive uncle. Of course, Toby was Robert's son, so that had strong resonances for me as well. We improvised and paraphrased. WE DID NOT BLOCK. And for the first few weeks, we sat in small groups, and learnt the lines, used them simply to talk to each other. That is what acting is all about for me. Working on your fellow actor and talking to him, not emoting, not doing anything for a planned effect, certainly not playing for laughs, but allowing the intention of the scene to emerge through the lines of your own determination to win your point.

It was a very happy time for me. I was drawn deeply into the character and given the freedom to explore it as much as I could. I was able to pursue several points of concentration without getting too much in the other actor's way. Food, drink, wit but above all – devotion to Coriolanus – the way I touched him – the way I defended him and so on.

There were exciting new developments taking place in the field of education at Stratford. The theatre itself had a busy education programme and eventually the Prince of Wales Summer School was established specifically for school teachers. But to begin with, I was invited to question and answer sessions at the Shakespeare Institute in Mason Croft and at the Birthplace Trust building in Henley Street. Nervous of them at first, they became a source of the greatest pleasure. Groups of students from this country and around the world under the guidance, usually, of Robert Smallwood, feed questions to the actor on the productions they have seen and we have to respond. To top it all, I was asked by Stanley Wells, in my second season, to talk for an hour to the annual Summer School at the Institute about Menenius and the way he was developed. A lecture! The room would be full of people who knew and cared about Shakespeare and about the RSC and the way it operates, so of course I was apprehensive. An actor talking about his work can be very precious! However the occasion was both exhilarating and rewarding and led the way to my giving a second lecture, on *Troilus and Cressida* when I returned in 1996.

Between the two talks, my experiences in the theatre had not been so rosy. I am uncomfortable when a directorial concept is applied to a play. My system is derailed when I have to jolt from one inconsistency to another, trying to accommodate the extraneous ideas which are forced upon the author's intentions. I had clashed with the director of *The Broken Heart*, and again, initially with the director of *The White Devil*. Ian Judge, *Troilus and Cressida* and Ulysses followed.

Ulysses, again, after thirty-six years. I met Ian Judge for the first time after he had cast me, during the sonnet readings given by younger company members on Shakespeare's birthday in The Swan foyer. 'You realize it's a comedy part', were his first words to me. A label. Already. Comedy business in the 'Degree' speech? Daunted, and a little resigned, I prepared as usual. My super-objective – for Ulysses that is – was to go home. After seven years of this abortive war, I just wanted to go home to my wife, Penelope, and my son. Well, I hung on to that, at least.

There were twenty-seven actors as opposed to thirty-seven in the 1960 production, so the Trojan and Greek armies were a little sparse. We sat around a table and worked on the script for three weeks cutting for sense and a little for length, and trying to understand it ... and then it was blocked ... or rather, CHOREOGRAPHED in a further three weeks. Great big circular moves and quite a few small figure-of-eights. Regardless of what we were trying to obtain from another character – off we would travel after a line or so to prevent the possibility of any boredom creeping in.

The look was all and the argument was secondary. Bare buttocks and leather with very little attention to the iambic pentameter. Sexual betrayal and heroic disillusionment traded for homo-eroticism and easy laughs and sold as such. No-one over forty was allowed to show any flesh and everything was subservient to the god – laughter! We all like to laugh and all actors like to get laughs, but if the gags are applied and don't emerge truly from the text, the audience isn't fooled. They may even laugh, but they're not fooled.

Our heroes were certainly debunked with feet of very ordinary clay, but many of the cast were left in limbo, which would erupt with unsettling flashes of mutiny. Ulysses gave me personally plenty to hang on to. A driving force, he is manipulative, cunning and cruel, and although I attempt to give him a human side, he remains a calculator and rather cold. I had intended to hinge my interpretation on his admiration for Troilus (enemies in sympathy – the father-son relationship) but that got lost in the interests of self-preservation.

In compensation, Ulysses has some of the finest verse in the language. Apart from the complex argument on degree and place in society, with all its violent imagery, he has the fabulously rich poetry and internal drama of the 'Time' speech. There are seventeen irregular lines, nine caesuras, and six end-stopped lines. Thirty-seven 'm's in forty-six lines – 'Made emulous missions 'mongst the Gods themselves and drave great Mars to faction'. Alliterative – it's a difficult consonant – lip exercises to make sure they're heard – 'calumniating time'. A huge intake of breath while Achilles asks, 'What, are my deeds forgot?', smiling at him the while, hitting the first word hard – it's a reverse stress – 'tum-ti-ti-tum', instead of 'ti-tum-ti-tum'. In quickly to deliver the first three lines in one breath. Shakespeare tells me when to pause. He gives three short lines at strategic points throughout, which give me time to wait for the meaning to dawn on the slow-witted Achilles – giving me time also to breathe. At the end of the speech – fourteen syllables including an interjection from Achilles. No pause. Fast. Pick up the cues. Almost an over-run. Naturalistic. Lower the diaphragm to gulp a vast amount of air, while Achilles asks, quickly, 'Ha! Known?'. Immediate response, accelerating the pace. Hammer home the points. Shame him as a traitor, then as a dishonourable father, and then onwards to the final monosyllabic line. 'The fool slides o'er the ice that you should break.' Deliberate. Hard. Slow. Equal stress like pistol shots. Then off and my blood is racing.

INTERLUDE

The Lost Gloves

KENNETH BRANAGH

On the following Monday we began the technical rehearsal. We were falling behind schedule, as the rehearsal
of lighting, sound and costume-changes was a time-consuming
affair. By the morning of the first preview on Thursday we had
still not finished, and there was a grave danger of not having a
dress rehearsal at all. This terrified me, as it was so long since
we had 'teched' the first scenes that we were all in danger of
forgetting everything. Adrian seemed to accept this as part of
the process but my mounting terror made me throw a mini-
wobbly. In a slightly shrill, hysterical falsetto I demanded the
chance to run the part before facing an audience. Adrian
breathed a heavy sigh. I wasn't the first queeny actor he'd run
across. At three o'clock that afternoon we started our first
dress rehearsal of the play. At 7.30 we did it again for the paying public. I went through the first performance in a daze. The
first time you play a large classical role your energies are completely absorbed in how to get on and off the stage, where your
costumes are, and how you can manage to drink a cup of tea

during the first half. Remembering and acting the lines seem to come a poor second. Rehearsal room revelations, psychological detail, conversations with prospective monarchs are all out of the window while the old pro inside you is screaming, 'How do I get off, love?'

All was fine until we'd won the Battle of Agincourt. I was wandering o'er the battlefield looking suitably moved and about to go into the scene with Fluellen and Williams where Henry sets up a complicated plot involving the exchange of gloves. Mine were supposed to be tucked into my belt, but weren't there. My crash course in Shakespearean paraphrase began there and then.

> Fluellen . . . as I do remember me,
> I bethinkst myself that I did have some gloves
> For which it was my full intent
> That thou shouldst with them work.
> But see alas, they are not here,
> Nor know I whenst they be.

By this stage every actor at the Battle of Agincourt was regarding their monarch with new amazement. From off-stage the noise of scurrying stage-management drifted onto the battlefield. There was no stopping me now – I had to get us out of this,

> Good Fluellen, although the gloves I do desire
> Be not here i' the field,
> My mind does't tell me of another pair
> That thou should'st find
> Were'st thou to look elsewhere.
> Be busy about this errand
> And return again I absolutely prithee.

Sion Probert, who was playing Fluellen, had turned green. What was I talking about? This wasn't what we'd rehearsed. He ran off-stage and as I continued through the interminable pause, marching around the battlefield, being (if it were possible) even more moved, I saw his arms waving up and down in the wings, and the Stage Manager whispering frantically, 'I haven't got any more fucking gloves.'

The moments passed and by this stage I had mourned individually over each of the Agincourt dead, and the shuddering shoulders of the English army told me that concentration was at an end. The air of perplexity coming off the audience was palpable. At last Sion ran back on carrying what looked like two motor-cycle gauntlets, and yelled.

I have found thy gloves, my liege.

A moment before I had spotted the original pair lying amongst the dead bodies. I had just snatched them up ready to carry on with the scene when the mad Welshman rushed on. Now the audience really were confused.

Well done, good fellow.
Thou does'st thy office fairly.
But I have found another pair
Which suiteth me more goodly.

Before I could wrench myself back onto the text I heard an audible 'Fuck me' from under Sion's breath. He clearly thought I'd done this on purpose. The rest of the show was performed on sheer adrenalin. The age that the gloves incident had seemed to take was clearly exaggerated by actually being part of it, but by the time I walked out of the theatre and to my car I was sure that the audience had not noticed.

I'd got through it, which was a huge relief, and Adrian was pleased. There was lots of work to do next day, but the reaction had been good and we'd got away with the one major embarrassment. As I opened the car door another vehicle drove past and the window was wound down. 'Superb, absolutely superb.'

That was nice. There, I knew we'd got away with it. They called again.

'Loved the gloves!'

* The Lost Gloves: an episode in Adrian Noble's production of *Henry V*, 1984

THE AUDIENCE

A Misspent Youth

MICHAEL BILLINGTON

I first visited the Stratford theatre in 1948. I was eight years old at the time and my parents, who lived in Leamington Spa, took me to see a production of *Troilus and Cressida*. Goodness knows what I made of it. But I remember being warned that the production was a bit unconventional: American military uniforms for the Greeks and a short lambswood jacket for Ulysses, though that may have been as much a reflection of post-war austerity as of avant-garde interpretation. I still have a clear recollection of specific scenes: most of all the one where Pandarus encourages Cressida to spy out Troilus ('What sneaking fellow comes yonder?') amongst the passing army. Only some years later did it dawn on me that I'd been lucky enough to see the young Paul Scofield as Troilus. The trip certainly bred a passion for Shakespeare: one fostered by a grandmother who constantly quoted Portia's 'The quality of mercy' speech and another aged female relative who, in quavering tones, would read aloud the Ghost's scenes from *Hamlet*. My parents were not well-off and my aged relatives were very much part of the impoverished working-class. Yet they could quote great chunks of Shakespeare which they presumably learned, by rote, at school. What's more they did so with love and passion: something worth remembering today when the idea that Shakespeare should be compulsorily taught in schools, and even learned by heart, is viewed with suspicion by educational progressives.

But it was my good luck to have been brought up near Stratford and to have had parents who actively encouraged my theatregoing. It was only in the 1950s, however, that I became fairly obsessive about Shakespeare and Stratford. I used to cycle the eight miles from Leamington to Stratford with a friend and – more often than not – get a standing-ticket at the back of the stalls for half-a-crown. Looking back it's fairly astonishing to think that I saw the cream of the British theatre in more or less the entire Shakespeare repertory for such a modest sum. Today, I notice, a standing-ticket costs a fiver: what is important, however, is that cheap seats remain available for the young, the hard-up and the dedicated.

What was the standard like at Stratford in the pre-RSC 1950s? The temptation is to wrap everything in nostalgia and to say it was all much better then. But firstly one should recall that in those days there was no Swan or Other Place: no chance to see the work of Shakespeare's contemporaries let alone Restoration, 19th century or modern plays. The basic diet was of five plays a season in the Memorial Theatre. Actors and directors came and went so there was also little sense of continuity. Also the standard of production was variable. I suspect that by the end of the 1950s the permutations of star-casting were beginning to be exhausted and the change was necessary and inevitable. Yet those 1950s seasons possessed a glamour and excitement that derived from the presence of actors such as Olivier, Gielgud, Redgrave and Ashcroft as well as directors of the calibre of Brook and Guthrie. It was Kenneth Tynan who wrote in 1952 that 'The safest introduction to the best in English theatre is still, for my money, the 2.10 from Paddington: change at Leamington for the shrine.'

Sadly, I missed much in the early 1950s: Burton's Prince Hal and Henry V, Ashcroft's Portia, Redgrave's Lear. I did, however, see Redgrave and Ashcroft together in *Antony and Cleopatra* in 1953: a Glen Byam Shaw production of extraordinary swiftness and clarity. Transitions from Rome to Alexandria were done with cinematic speed. A rope looped with canvas indicated Pompey's galley. Two purple poles suggested Octavia's court. Above all, there were two great performances. Redgrave's Antony, with his commanding height and melodious voice, was a ruined Titan. Ashcroft's Cleopatra, who made a running entrance with Antony tethered to her by a long rope of water-lilies, was all mercurial volatility and passion: with her ponytail wig and plunging neckline she seemed, to my youthful eyes, the embodiment of rapturous sexuality.

It was in 1955, however, that I became a Stratford devotee. It was partly because I was taking my O-levels that year and one of my set-texts, *Macbeth*, was in the repertory: I went at least three times. But I was also drawn by the sheer star-power of the Oliviers who, to a somewhat solitary Leamington teenager, seemed like creatures from another world. My first sight of Olivier himself was as Malvolio in Gielgud's rather cold, prettified *Twelfth Night*. I was, in truth, a touch disappointed: Olivier, in his search for an image to convey Malvolio's outsiderness, played him rather like a camp Jewish hairdresser. But there were some inventive touches: when he came to the word 'slough' Olivier experimented with the pronunciation as if unsure whether it should rhyme with 'rough' or 'row.' And his final exit was unforgettable with his cry of 'I'll be revenged on the whole pack of you' reverberating through the play's final moments.

About Olivier's *Macbeth*, however, there was no equivocation. This was the thing itself: the kind of great acting that sent a thrill down the spine. One quality that lingers with me still is Olivier's dark, ironic humour: the scene with the two murderers was full of saturnine mockery with Olivier picking up unexpected laughs on 'Ay, in the catalogue ye go for men.' But there was also the soul-searing pathos, much written about by Harold Hobson, of 'My way of life is fallen into the sere, the yellow leaf' and the sudden soar on 'troops of friends' as if this *Macbeth* was painfully conscious of the cost of tyranny and of his own echoing isolation. It was also my first glimpse of Olivier's magnetic animalism: on 'Lay on Macduff' he pawed the ground with his feet like a bull waiting to enter the arena. Years later I became friends with Olivier's Banquo, Ralph Michael, who told me how he had to enter in downstage darkness while Olivier himself posed on a small, suspiciously well-lit crag. But, even if Olivier was not the most generous of actors, he was still a towering Macbeth.

The other triumph that season was Peter Brook's production of *Titus Andronicus* with the Oliviers: I got a standing-ticket for the first night and somewhere still have a programme with a black cover that marked the occasion. Odd to recall that the play was then virtually unknown and regarded as barely performable: now it is regularly revived and looks like Shakespeare's first masterpiece. Brook's production was also like nothing I had ever seen in the theatre: a piece of ritual full of slow processions, hieratic priests, musique concrète, stylised colours including bold reds and greens. And Olivier himself turned Titus into a gnarled, leathery soldier with seamed face who gradually achieved a Lear-like stature. Once again, I was struck by Olivier's comic instinct: in the first scene he whipped up applause for the emperor and then just as quickly damped it down again. Yet Olivier played the great central passages with the surging emotion of a man driven mad by grief. Journalistically, the production became famous for the number of people who fainted when Titus chopped off his hand to the sound of crunching bone. What was really impressive, however, was the extent to which Brook stylised the cruelty so that even the rape and mutilation of Lavinia, played by Vivien Leigh, became aesthetically bearable.

After the excitements of the Olivier season, there was a slight air of anti-climax about 1956; though I remember a good, robust Othello from Harry Andrews, a pillar of Stratford in the 1950s, and a rather formal, geometrically elegant production of *Love's Labour's Lost* from Peter Hall (his Stratford début) that quickened into life with the arrival of Mark Dignam's Holofernes, cackling out his Latin tags as if they were catchphrases from ITMA. But I seem to have spent a lot of the spring and summer of 1957 cycling to Stratford: this time because I was studying *King John* for A-Levels and the play was, very considerately, in the repertoire. Whenever I ask why this particular play is cold-shouldered today, and hardly ever played in the main-house, I am told it is because it is box-office poison; yet I have a sharp memory of seeing it seven or eight times in 1957 and always with packed, enthusiastic houses.

Douglas Seale, the director, animated it beautifully: the abiding image was of sombre darkness lit by flickering torches.

The Hubert-Arthur scenes, in particular, grew out of the crepuscular background and were played with searing intensity by Ron Haddrick (who had played cricket for South Australia and went on to become one of the country's top actors) and the young Christopher Bond. Although we talk a lot today about verse-speaking and the need for actors to understand the importance of caesura and end-stopped lines, what I recall most sharply from that production is the inherent musicality of the voices: most of all the iron gravity of Robert Harris's King and the golden mellifluousness of Alec Clunes's Bastard. I don't think it is just middle-aged romanticism to suggest that there was a resonant vocal richness in the 1950s which is harder to find today: maybe it has something to do with the anti-verbal nature of our culture. Modern actors are, I am sure, much better trained in the art of verse-speaking: that, however, cannot compensate for declining standards in public speech or the gradual impoverishment of the language.

Without dwindling into nostalgia, one should also point out that Stratford productions of the 1950s were, at their best, very good indeed. In 1957 there was a beautiful, if visually cluttered, *Cymbeline* from Peter Hall that enshrined Peggy Ashcroft's ardent, impossibly youthful Imogen. Peter Brook also directed *The Tempest*, with Gielgud as Prospero, in a style that re-defined both the play and the central character. The bareness of the stage – and I have an image of Peter Johnson's Ferdinand lugging logs from its topmost point – showed Brook reaching towards his ideal of 'the empty space.' Gielgud's Prospero was also deliberately de-romanticised: he sported a torso-revealing hessian cloth and was an angry, nut-brown hermit rather than the conventional heavily draped Jasper Maskelyne. Gielgud also belied his reputation as simply being a golden larynx: he used the language to reveal character. I can still hear the escalating anger of 'Though with their high wrongs I am struck to the quick' modulating into the softer-toned 'Yet, with my nobler reason, 'gainst my fury, Do I take part.' I always thought it one of Gielgud's best performances and Brook's finest productions.

By now, however, my own life was changing and my visits to Stratford became marginally less frequent. In the autumn of 1958 I went up to Oxford to read English: a choice of subject partly dictated, I am sure, by my passion for Shakespeare. Even in that year, however, I did get to see Redgrave's Hamlet three times. What that taught me was how unfair it is that actors are always judged by their first nights. Redgrave was a notoriously uncertain starter and his first night performance was imbued with an hysteria that often seemed technically uncontrolled. By the autumn his Hamlet had become a thing of beauty: intelligence, reflectiveness, nobility were all there but so too was a throttled ineffectual intensity (qualities Redgrave later used in his *Uncle Vanya*). Redgrave was around 50 when he played the part; but age, as with Ashcroft, seemed irrelevant when so much else was right. I have seen countless Hamlets since; but none has moved me as much as Redgrave or given so complete a picture of the multifariousness of Hamlet's character. That same season he was also a remarkable Benedick whose voice hit a strange falsetto note on 'Man is a giddy creature' as if mutability were the essential clue to the character.

My perspective on Stratford changed somewhat in 1959: I actually performed there. One excellent idea that took root in the late 1950s was to invite student companies to perform non-Shakespearian classics in the gardens behind the theatre: the kind of work, in fact, for which The Swan was later built. As a playgoer I'd seen a brilliant Marlowe Society production of

Edward II and an indifferent OUDS *All For Love.* And in my
first year at Oxford I signed on for a production of *Bartholomew
Fair* lured by the prospect of a summer tour to Leicester and
Stratford. My own role was a modest one: not quite as modest,
however, as that of Dudley Moore who played an itinerant
apple-seller. But the production, co-directed by Ken Loach in
his pre-political days, was a lively one and included a delightful
moment when Justice Overdo (played by Peter Holmes who
later became a professional actor and then schoolteacher) was
hurled into the Avon. My chief memory, however, is of some
very good summer parties and of the conviviality of the Stratford company. We didn't get to meet Laughton, Robeson or
Olivier who were all playing at Stratford that year but we did
rub shoulders with Vanessa Redgrave, Diana Rigg, Albert
Finney, Paul Hardwick, Peter Woodthorpe and somehow felt
that we were, if not actually in the company, at least obliquely
associated with it.

That season, billed as the 100th, was a star-studded affair and
it exhibited both the strengths and weaknesses of Stratford in
the 1950s. It yielded some individually magnificent performances and productions. But they were not bound together by
any sense of internal consistency or what we would call today
a 'house-style.' Merry eclecticism was the order of the day; but
it was clear that Stratford could not go on for ever repeating
the pattern of what a contemporary radio series called 'The
stars in their choices.'

Olivier's Coriolanus, in Peter Hall's production, was the
great performance of that season; and I never see the play
today without it coming to mind. People still talk of the famous
moment when Olivier, in death, dangled upside down in final
Mussolini-like ignominy. But what I recall is his brilliant display

of Coriolanus's emotional immaturity: forced to confront his wife in the market-place he rolled his eyes in schoolboyish embarrassment and, when Aufidius hurled the phrase 'thou boy of tears' at him, he echoed the word 'boy' with a fierce and savage anger. Olivier, as always, was also a great ironist: in the scene where Volumnia and Menenius attempt to placate him before he re-encounters the tribunes and the people, Olivier played every possible variation on the word 'mildly' barking it out with rebarbative scorn before silently mouthing it on his exit as if to highlight the character's adolescent nature. It is the sound, as well as the sight, of an Olivier performance that stays with one: on 'Your enemies with nodding of their plumes fan you into despair' Olivier lingered on the last word as if conjuring up the emotion it described. That is the kind of creative intelligence that I suspect no academy can teach. But the most joyous production of that particular season was Guthrie's *All's Well That Ends Well* set in a timeless Edwardian world that shaded into Army Game antics for the Parolles scenes. Guthrie was an extraordinary director. No-one could choreograph a crowd better or produce single moments of such heart-stopping brilliance: when Robert Hardy's King of France, cured of the fistula, waltzed into the court with Zoe Caldwell's Helena it was as if we had just witnessed some miracle-cure renewing life and energy. And, even though it was always claimed that Guthrie shied away from emotion, my memory is of the scenes between Edith Evans's Countess and Caldwell's Helena radiating a pure Chekhovian humanity. In later years I saw a handful of Guthrie productions at Nottingham, Bristol and in the West End. What he brought to the theatre was not simply fluidity of movement but a heightened sense of the medium's potential: an awareness of the theatreness of theatre. His antithesis today is a director like Jonathan Miller who, for all his obvious intelligence, treats plays as if they were academic exercises and seems not to enjoy the presentional aspect of theatre.

By 1960 Stratford was ready for change. The creation of the Royal Shakespeare Company, with its emphasis on continuity, permanence and a collective attitude to verse-speaking, was an historical necessity. So I am not one of those who sigh for a return to some mythical golden era: indeed I would say the RSC has erred largely when it has strayed from Peter Hall's first principles and become an eclectic institution subject to all kinds of directional influence. But the Shakespeare Memorial Theatre, in the era of Anthony Quayle and Glen Byam Shaw, was a remarkable institution that rescued Stratford from the charge of provincial mediocrity and that gave Shakespearian acting and production an almost sexual glamour and excitement. In raking through my memories of star-performances I have also neglected to mention the very fine work that was done by Stratford regulars: people like Patrick Wymark who was much more than a moon-faced clown, Mark Dignam whose every performance had a hard-edged authority, Anthony Nicholls who exuded patrician dignity.

For someone of my generation, Stratford Shakespeare in the 1950s was both a constant source of pleasure and a theatrical education. It taught me about the plays. It also left behind an ineradicable set of images and sounds. And, unconsciously, I suspect it determined my choice of career. Even then I used to come home from the theatre and write up, in an exercise book, my impressions of the plays and performances; and much of the impulse to become a critic stemmed from that desire to pin down an evanescent art. So Stratford today is constantly haunted by the ghosts of the past. And, while one should never become a slave to one's memories and use them as a stick with which to beat the present, it is also valuable to retain them and see new interpretations in some kind of historical context. But, if there is one lesson that can be learned from that period, it is that Stratford's main house has a moral duty to stage the whole canon. What worries me today is the assumption that certain plays – *King John, Henry VIII, Timon of Athens, Pericles* – are essentially chamber-works of limited audience appeal. No such assumption was made in the 1950s or indeed in the early years of the RSC. And, if I could recapture one thing from the past, it would be the desire to make the entire Shakespeare canon available on the main stage. But I have no wish to look back in dewy-eyed nostalgia. For me, and others of my theatregoing generation, the 1950s was a lucky decade in which to be alive. But I assume, and fervently hope, that there are still young people today for whom playgoing at Stratford is not just a scholastic duty but a source of personal excitement. Indeed when I look round the faces at the Royal Shakespeare Theatre or The Swan I know that to be so. The cycle of discovery endlessly continues.

'As I remember ... it was upon this fashion ...'

LORNA FLINT

To encounter, all for the first time, and all on the same day, Shakespeare's Stratford, Shakespeare's Theatre, and Shakespeare's *King Lear* might well make on anyone, even in 1997, a considerable impression. On me, in 1936, the effect proved indelible. Komisarjevski's production, Randle Ayrton's performance, and the revelation of a cyclorama combined to convince me, even then, that one day Shakespeare and Stratford would provide my permanent earthly paradise. Sixty years on, they still do.

But that startling performance of *King Lear* had to sustain me, almost unaided, for the next ten years. The war, and the strictures of a student's grants, severely rationed theatre-going. A rare Stratford visit has left with me the memory of a rare performance: Patricia Jessell's enchanting Viola; but it was not until 1945 that Stratford Festivals became an annual event for me, and it was during this season that I first began to appreciate the actors' remarkable versatility. It was extraordinary to see Claire Luce as a dangerously seductive Cleopatra on my first night, Viola Lyell as a poignant Queen Katherine on the second, and then both of them as the merriest of Merry Wives on the third – with David Read as the funniest Master Slender I have ever seen. His petulant, exasperated 'What need you tell me that?' when Master Page pointed out that he had been mistaken in taking 'a great lubberly boy' for 'sweet Anne Page' moved a delighted audience to a burst of spontaneous applause; but next night, in *Much Ado About Nothing*, his Don John – menacingly black-clad, icy-voiced, pallid, with a paralyzed left arm, its long-fingered hand laden with glittering rings – sent shivers down the spine. It was a season full of promise, richly fulfilled in 1946. For now the war was over. Sir Barry Jackson was appointed as Director; there was more time to spend on rehearsals, and more money too, to spend on the productions. Although utility curtain-sets had never bothered me, so long as I could see and hear the actors (which, whatever is said now about the disastrous short-comings of the main house, I always could) I was satisfied. All the same, it was exhilarating to see the great front curtain swing back to reveal a radiant, magical island for *The Tempest*, and later an elegant Watteau-styled set and costumes for *Love's Labour's Lost*. My impression is that most of this season's plays were open to air and sky. They let in the light. They also let in new, young actors, one of whom in particular – Paul Scofield – was instantly taken to Stratford's discerning heart. It was a season that offered what I can best, if paradoxically, describe as steady excitement. Every play made a distinct, individual impression. It is only now that I have come upon the likely reason: for the first time, there was a different director for each of the seven plays. Of the seven productions, it is *Macbeth* that has made the strongest impression. It was quite the most entertaining *Macbeth* I have ever seen, and for all the wrong reasons. Why is it that most of its directors cannot resist saddling the actors of a play notoriously acknowledged to be difficult to stage with the additional hazard of every kind of step and stair? The 1946 production crammed the stage with enormous staircases, one on each side, so that most of the cast were on the move most of the time. Never has Macbeth's 'That is a step/On which I must fall down or else o'er-leap,/For in my way it lies' been more feelingly spoken than it was by Robert Harris. One watched, riveted, to see which alternative he would choose. From then on, the audience did its loyal best to stifle its chuckles. But those wretched staircases upstaged everyone. However, Robert Harris came into his own as Prospero. His spell-binding vocal music echoed the beauty of the set, just as the visual charm of Peter Brook's *Love's Labour's Lost* was audibly matched in the skilful balancing of the lovers' witty repartee, the robust self-confidence of the comic characters, and the wistfulness (a hall-mark of so many of Paul Scofield's performances) of a mistakenly complacent Armado.

History books record Sir Barry Jackson's vigorous and comprehensive spring-cleaning, when he became the Festival Director in 1946, but I, for one, was not consciously aware of what was going on behind the scenes. It was the scenes themselves that claimed my attention. Four of the 1947 productions were revivals, but of the five new ones, two have left indelible marks – and distinctly black ones, so far as Peter Brook's acclaimed *Romeo and Juliet* was concerned. It was my first experience of a production that wantonly crippled a play by imposing on the audience the director's whims at the expense of Shakespeare's text. The cutting of the dialogue between Friar Laurence and Juliet was irritating enough, and made the subsequent plot

difficult to follow; but to abolish the Chorus's promise of re-
conciliation between Capulet and Montague was to destroy the
play's integrity. One other production was considerably cut,
but excusably so: Nugent Monck's *Pericles*. No-one could argue
that Shakespeare was being betrayed when his authorship was
uncertain; and the theme and plot did not suffer severely.
Inevitably, it was Paul Scofield's performance as Pericles that
stayed in the mind – that, and the satisfaction of seeing a play
so rarely performed.

While some of this season's most successful productions
travelled on to London in 1948, Stratford provided innova-
tions on two fronts. First, there were no revivals in the theatre;
nine brand-new productions were on offer. But the second
innovation was to become a cherished institution: the estab-
lishing of the Theatre Summer School. During my 1946 and
1947 visits, I had discovered, as I did again in 1948, that there
were lectures to enjoy, as well as plays. But I had no idea that
this time I was invading the first Summer School – the Theatre
Summer School, run by John Garrett, and sponsored by the
Shakespeare Memorial Theatre, the University of Birmingham,
and the Shakespeare Birthplace Trust. I have never missed one
since.

1948 was a splendid year for the Summer School's inaug-
uration. The company included past favourites, but was
strengthened by Sir Barry Jackson's importation of recognized
stars – for instance, Diana Wynyard, Robert Helpmann, Es-
mond Knight, Godfrey Tearle. Their presence in itself stirred
up any audience's expectations, even for an opening production as unfamiliar as *King John*. The choice of Robert Helpmann
for the King – all dark, unpredictable menace, expressed in sin-
uous grace – and of Anthony Quayle for the Bastard – equally

shrewd, but with a build and stance and humorous charm that won all hearts – was inspired casting. Indeed, the conflicts of such contrasts were the core of this season's successes: obvious contrasts, between Helpmann's dangerous, feline Shylock and Diana Wynyard's golden serene Portia; between the court and the country scenes in *The Winter's Tale*; between – even more obviously – Petruchio and Katherine in *The Taming of the Shrew*, and Greeks and Trojans in *Troilus and Cressida*. Within such broad generalization, specific details stand proud. There were moments of such perfect timing and phrasing in *Troilus and Cressida* that I hear them again whenever I see the play: Hector's incredulous 'I am unarmed; forgo this vantage, Greek' when Achilles entered with his Myrmidons – an honourable soldier's utter inability to believe that another professional could take so contemptible an advantage; and Agamemnon's delicate timing, sharing the joke with his spectators both on and off stage, when he modulated his outrageous praise of the gullible Ajax's virtues to a heartfelt aside – 'and altogether more tractable'. One heard, in those four words, all the pressures on a king and commander, having to keep his awkward troops in some sort of civilized order. There are too many heights and depths of language, philosophy, comedy and tragedy in *Troilus and Cressida* for any production to satisfy fully everyone's expectations. But this one left me full of excitement, and sent me straight back to the text.

But it was in the production of *Hamlet* that the greatest of the season's risks were taken. Michael Benthall dared to double-cast Hamlet himself. Robert Helpmann and Paul Scofield played the Prince alternately, and it was of course essential to see both performances, and to compare and contrast them, and it was of course inevitable that people who could not see

both felt cheated. To my surprise, I found Helpmann's interpretation more arresting than Scofield's. The intelligence and
authority that Helpmann brought to the part seemed to me
more convincing, more capable of sustaining its variety and
weight, than Scofield's pitiable vulnerability. He was not helped
by the second daring experiment – to put the play into Victor-
ian dress. On him, it was fancy dress, whereas Helpmann could
make any costume entirely his own. The rest of the cast adapted themselves to their nineteenth-century embellishments
and their alternating Princes with admirable ease; so much so,
that the production's eccentricities turned what can so easily
seem a tiresome self-indulgence on the director's part into a
means of illumination. One particular touch of characteriza-
tion had that effect on me: the sight of Anthony Quayle's very
slightly unsteady Claudius, glass in hand, justifying Hamlet's
contempt for a King who constantly 'takes his rouse'.

The most important event for the Theatre in 1949, when Sir
Barry Jackson retired, must have been Anthony Quayle's
appointment – not just of the festival season, but as the first
Director of the Theatre. But it was the season itself that interested me, though only its final production has left a lasting,
clear impression. It took Tyrone Guthrie's *Henry VIII* to bring
out the best in every member of the cast. He was only the second producer (Komisarjevski having been the first) whose
name I registered at once, and never forgot. Thanks to the
splendour and variety of his *Henry VIII*, and to the re-charged
energy of the company, a season which had begun in a minor,
if not a low, key ended with a flourish.

After four years' steady attendance at the Festivals and the
available lectures, I arrived at the 1950 season just as eagerly,
but more critically, than before. For the first time, the Theatre

Summer School programme included a lecturer from within the company: one who was prepared to share with us the kinds of problems his work entailed. Anthony Quayle's 'On Producing Shakespeare', answering our unspoken questions, stimulated a conscious interest in all that contributed to the performances that an audience, reasonably enough, took for granted. From now on, Directors (replacing 'Producer' on programmes for the first time), musicians, designers, craftsmen, actors, began to emerge from their previous seclusion and anonymity. I remember how privileged we felt when, abandoning the usual practice of secrecy, Anthony Quayle divulged his plans for 1951. That season was to consist of a series of English History plays, acted in a permanent scaffolding set which would, he hoped, retain the essential factors of an Elizabethan stage. Meanwhile, the 1950 programme was one to savour. It was a wonderful season for voices: Gielgud's remote as Angelo, urgent as Cassius, stretched heart-breakingly to run the gamut as *King Lear*, Harry Andrews's – measured as the play's title as *Measure for Measure*'s Duke, gravely sententious as Brutus, alive to the changing roles as Edgar; Anthony Quayle's – by turns boisterously good-humoured and dangerously brusque as Henry VIII, master of rhetorical tricks as Mark Antony; Peggy Ashcroft's – quietly 'gentle' yet resolute as Cordelia. Such confidence, range, and intelligence are not so often found in such abundance today. This season more than compensated for the shortcomings of 1949.

Anthony Quayle's announcement that 1951 was to be (almost) confined to four English History plays, all on the same set, each with the same actor carrying his part throughout the season, had caused a stir in the Summer School when he made it. Some were disappointed, foreseeing monotony.

Others were curious, wondering how it would work. In fact, during this centenary Festival of Britain year, it was an acknowledged success. As a tactful counterweight, there was a truly magical *Tempest* – a play in itself as various as anyone could wish. I loved this production. The curtain rose on waves of gauzy sea-nymphs; the music was harmonious charmingly; the clowns were of the earth, earthy; the goddesses in the Masque (Barbara Jefford spectacularly splendid as 'great Juno') descended smoothly from the flies; Caliban (Hugh Griffiths) was allowed to play for pathos; Ariel (Alan Badel) miraculously embodied his name; the royal party, gorgeous in their wedding garments, well deserved Miranda's 'How beauteous mankind is!' Michael Redgrave had all the attributes one could wish for as Prospero: commanding height, a graceful presence, a voice capable of striking amazement when he exerted his power, but capable always of savouring the poetry. Whether one had chosen to see Michael Benthall's production as an appetizer or as a bonne bouche to the History cycle, it was a complete feast in itself.

But critical focus was naturally fixed on the historical experiment. In Stratford, Parts 1 and 2 of *Henry IV* had only once before (in 1932) been played in sequence, and since then there had been no performance of Part 2, and only one (in 1935) of Part 1. The plays were clearly less popular than the comedies and tragedies, and they were certainly not among my favourites. So I owe a great debt to Anthony Quayle, to his co-Directors (John Kidd and Michael Redgrave), and to the firmly knit company of actors who opened my eyes and ears to what I had been missing. Of all the King Richards I have seen, Michael Redgrave's, every inch of his six feet three inches a king, whether in glory or in misery, remains my favourite. It

was only when I realized that he would later be working his
particular magic not only as Prospero, but also as the Chorus
in *Henry V*, and the engaging, crackling Northumbrian Hotspur in *1 Henry IV*, that I was reconciled to his death in *Richard
II*. The main weight of the cycle was magnificently carried by
Harry Andrews. To follow his development from Bolingbroke,
the ominously self-contained subject, to the royal, ruthless
usurper, and finally to the disillusioned weariness of an over-
burdened mortal creature was enough to convince any initially
unenthusiastic theatre-goer that the bold experiment of the
history sequence was worth the risk. The fall and rise of
Richard Burton's Prince Hal provided one of the counterbal-
ances which made the sheer narrative of the plays so power-
fully engrossing. In one way, this narrative emphasis changed
the impact of Falstaff. In the sweep of such a continuous pressure of events, he and his vastly entertaining episodes became
variations on the plays' serious themes, instead of the dominating figure he is often expected to be. Anthony Quayle, as
co-Director of Part 1, as well as the Falstaff in both parts, rightly put himself into the perspective of the whole cycle. All the
characters and all their actors, making their exits and their
entrances with such intelligent discretion, superbly contributed
to a season in which the parts – in every sense – worked together to form the triumphant whole. And to crown it, Britain's
Festival year included, at the end, the award of CBE to
Anthony Quayle.

It would not have been surprising if the 1952 season had
come as something of an anticlimax. That it did not was, in
part, due to the presentation of a programme skilfully designed
to include a popular revival – *The Tempest*; three new productions – *Coriolanus*, *As You Like It*, and *Macbeth*; and another nov-

elty – Ben Jonson's *Volpone*. A second stimulus was the arrival of Glen Byam Shaw. During the year, he was appointed as co-Director with Anthony Quayle, and their fruitful collaboration, leading eventually to Byam Shaw's sole directorship, when Quayle resigned in 1956, provided the most successfully sustained period of excellence that the theatre has ever known.

Glen Byam Shaw's first production, and the first of the season, was *Coriolanus*. Anthony Quayle, with his sturdy frame, immense self-confidence, and resonant voice, was the epitome of fearless arrogance; yet the boyish look that he never entirely outgrew, together, no doubt, with his audiences' affection for him, allowed his Coriolanus to win for this usually unsympathetic hero an understanding first justified, in the text, by the underlying humour in his dialogue with Volumnia – 'Mother, I am going to the market-place./Chide me no more./Look, I am going ...' His performance convinced me that Shakespeare meant Coriolanus to be played by an actor who either was or could look young. In this production, Michael Hordern's Menenius, with years of diplomacy behind him, proved the perfect foil to Coriolanus's tactless, ruthless implacability. Glen Byam Shaw's always happy partnership with Motley, as designer, combined with his imaginative lighting and convincing crowd scenes, launched the season with both polish and vigour. He opened his *As You Like It* (and later his *Merry Wives*) with an innovation now taken for granted. Motley's set revealed the chill of winter, matching man's ingratitude, until Oliver's jealous treatment of his brother, the dangerous entertainment of the wrestling, and Duke Frederick's abrupt banishment of his innocent niece, were left behind, and Spring arrived in the forest of Arden. This sure, unobtrusive interpretation of Shakespeare's text was characteristic of all Byam

Shaw's productions. When the *As You Like It* cast changed for the 1953 revival, I welcomed Peggy Ashcroft and Richard Johnson as Rosalind and Orlando, but the production itself needed no recycling. Byam Shaw's response to a text was not to impose on it alien eccentricities, but to see that his actors developed their individuality from the situations they were in and the words they spoke. For instance: his Adam and Corin shared the common characteristics of old age, but their appearances, actions, and voices distinguished clearly between the nervous, hand-wringing servant of a tyrant's household and the sturdy, relaxed self-confidence of the countryman, ready to speak openly of his master's 'churlish disposition' and hold his own against Touchstone's raillery. The directing that could make memorable and three-dimensional such comparatively minor characters still astonishes me. *As You Like It* was Glen Byam Shaw's favourite among the comedies, and the loving attention he paid to every aspect of it made one see why.

After the delight inspired by this production, Ralph Richardson's performance in John Gielgud's production of *Macbeth* came as a sad anticlimax. It was difficult to see exactly why. There were no outright calamities, like those in the disastrous 1946 production – not, anyway, when I saw it. It was simply inert. Ralph Richardson, rather than Macbeth, seemed unhappy throughout, and though the rest of the cast did what it could, the performance remained a beast without a heart. It was a huge relief to see Richardson revelling in a part well suited to his wonderful comic resources when he appeared as Volpone Anthony Quayle transformed himself into an extraordinarily Uriah Heep-like Mosca; Michael Hordern reduced the audience to hilarious tears with his tortured, tortoise antics as Sir Politic Would-Be; and a good time was had by all. I trea-

sure the memory of an unrehearsed moment, when Anthony
Quayle's slimy Mosca was obliged for an instant to become
Anthony Quayle's dashing Coriolanus: the sliding panel of
Volpone's treasure-chest stuck, and Mosca took a sword to it,
with a swashing and instantly applauded blow. When the Festival Season ended for the Stratford audiences, the Company
split itself in two. One half, under Anthony Quayle's direction,
set off on a tour to Australia and New Zealand. The other half,
left in Glen Byam Shaw's hands, began preparations for the
1953 season.

I have left myself with no space to do justice to the first four
productions, though each has left me with vidid memories. But
the crown of this Festival, which to my mind has never been
dislodged, was awarded by common, and even critical, consent
to Glen Byam Shaw's production of *Antony and Cleopatra*. From
the glittering blaze of Cleopatra's entourage, on which the curtain rose, to the single, dimming shaft of light focussed on her
throne of death, the play held the audience in thrall. Expecta-
tion and surprise in turn satisfied and amazed. Sights and
sounds, actions and reactions, comedy and tragedy – all were
so subtly and compellingly woven in the presentation of the
play's huge span that we became participants rather than spectators and auditors; and it was only in retrospect that one could
begin to appreciate the parts that made up the spell-binding
whole. Then, one could marvel at the brilliant and hitherto
unsuspected range of Peggy Ashcroft's irresistible Cleopatra,
and understand both the charismatic power and the subjuga-
tion of Michael Redgrave's Antony. The political intricacies of
the play were constantly clarified by the timing of speech and
action – when, for instance, the simplest, briefest snatch of dialogue – 'Welcome to Rome./Thank you./Sit./Sit, sir./Nay

then' – between Octavius Caesar and Antony pointed the danger underlying this superficially comical, musical-chairs confrontation, uneasily chaired by the ineffectual Lepidus, and undermined by Enobarbus's role of ironic commentator. The same marrying of Shakespeare's economy and the actors' timing set one's teeth on edge when Octavius quenched his eager, affectionate, sister's greeting on her return to Rome – 'Hail, Caesar, and my lord: hail, most dear Caesar!' – with a response – 'that ever I should call thee castaway!' – so devastatingly delivered that it chilled the theatre. Then there was the incredible moment when, without any words at all, Cleopatra and her treasurer, simply by a look, made it clear that they had arranged in advance how to mislead Caesar over the disposal of her wealth. Plutarch's account makes this explicit; but how Cleopatra, Seleucus, and Glen Byam Shaw between them conveyed it from the vast stage of the Memorial Theatre, I do not know. I know only that they did. Such delicate, penetrating touches of direction were of course subordinated to the great tableaux and confrontations of the production, but they made life-like – credible – the larger-than-life aspects of the play. And at the end, when the Romans, clad all through in frigid shades of grey, white and black, stood back from the fading blaze of Cleopatra robed and crowned, it seemed as though Cleopatra's prediction – 'I shall show the cinders of my spirits/Through the ashes of my chance' – was simultaneously true and false. The triumphant Roman power, cold and hard as iron, had choked the flames to ashes; but in this production, Shakespeare and Glen Byam Shaw left us with more than cinders. People quite often ask, 'Which is your favourite Shakespeare play?'; and if I had any doubts before I saw this production, I have had none since. Glen Byam Shaw's *Antony and Cleopatra* remains a revelation, and my greatest theatrical experience.

In the years that followed, it was bricks and mortar that were to bring about the greatest theatrical developments. Forty years ago, overnight visitors – granted co-operative transport – could fit in three Shakespeare performances at the Festival Theatre. Today, the same three visitors can still fit in three plays, but they will be at three different theatres; and only at the RST can they be sure to find Shakespeare. At the Swan, there may be a play by Ben Jonson, or a Restoration dramatist, or a translation; at The Other Place, there will be something new, or experimental, or both. The existence of the three theatres has completely changed the Festival pattern; but together they have kept the RSC on the theatrical map. Audiences at home and abroad are now experiencing live Shakespeare for the first time, while in Stratford, hitherto Shakespeare-only audiences are enjoying plays they never even knew existed. Freed from a proscenium arch, and with stage (or 'space') thrust into the audience, actors have learned how to develop a close relationship with their patrons, and among themselves. The new theatres have spread their wings, and soared.

I wish the main house had done so too. It continues to fly, but its course is uncertain. Its directors seem to have lost their predecessors' art of fusing text and performance so as to exploit the impressive dimensions of the space at their disposal. Their actors need to be rather larger than life: otherwise, when they play for subtlety they dwindle into nonentity. To make and maintain an impact, they need the strengthening support of tactful, bone-defining make-up, well-structured tailoring, free gesture, and confident carriage. Most of all, they need the freedom to interpret the plays unhindered by directorial additions, subtractions, or misinterpretations, which distract attentive audiences 'though in the mean time some necessary question of the play be then to be considered'. Hamlet's advice is not always followed in the RST. But when it is, it too can achieve greatness.

Remembering my early experiences, I wondered which productions during the last three-and-a-half seasons have immediately made me feel 'I must see this again'. I knew at once: at the RST, *Twelfth Night* and *Henry V* in 1994; at the Swan, *Coriolanus* in 1994 and *Henry VIII* – or *All is True* – in 1997; at The Other Place, *The Comedy of Errors* in 1996. If, miraculously, my hypothetical overnight visitors could have seen any three of these, they would surely not have departed without booking their next year's accommodation. For every season offers the thrilling possibility that, in one of the three theatres, they too may discover their greatest theatrical experience in a production performed by 'The best actors in the world'.

Playgoing

MARGARET YORKE

The play's the thing, and so it is.

Theatre is magic. It has always been important to me: the moment when the lights dimmed and the curtain, that fourth wall, rose to reveal the secrets it concealed was always thrilling; today there is rarely a curtain, but there is sometimes a veil, hinting at mystery, and the spell is cast.

Stratford and its theatre entered my life in 1950, when I moved to a village a few miles away. At the time this fact was irrelevant; the object was to be within commuting distance of Birmingham. Though I already loved the theatre – what little I had seen – like so many, I had been put off Shakespeare while at school. There, *Macbeth* was thrust at me to be dissected, its speeches learned by heart after first being read aloud in class, where, a shy girl, I dreaded being chosen to deliver Lady Macbeth's most embarrassing remarks. At that age I had seen none of the plays except, when I was very young and living in Dublin, a performance of *A Midsummer Night's Dream*. I was rather fond of donkeys, and was alarmed by Bottom in his ass's head. I can still recall my scared bewilderment, and long after I became a convert I had reservations about that play – which, it must be agreed, has a confusing plot, with three of the main female characters bearing names beginning with H. Peter Brook's production in 1970 was a revelation; after the first few startled minutes, I was entranced: all, at last, became clear. Later, I saw that production again in London, with a group of schoolboys aged twelve and thirteen. The boys had earlier performed, out of doors, Act One of *Julius Caesar*, and their spirited acting had been enhanced by the man tending the swimming pool who, by coincidence, caused the water to boil and bubble just before the reference to the Tiber trembling was uttered. The boys laughed a great deal during the *Dream*, and then, in the interval, one of them asked anxiously if Shakespeare would have been shocked to hear their merriment. Attitudes had not changed over the years, it seemed, as I assured them that he would have been delighted; the plays, I pointed out, had been written to be enjoyed.

My own fascination with the theatre began when I was nine and saw James Barrie's *Mary Rose* with Jean Forbes-Robertson. To me, it was so real: I was there, hovering ghost-like near that island, hearing her being summoned. Then there were pantomimes and *Peter Pan* – Jean Forbes-Robertson again – and later, occasionally, Coward and Rattigan plays, perhaps a revue or a musical. My visits to the theatre in Stratford during the golden years of Anthony Quayle's directorship were initiated by my cousin. While I had been immured in Solihull with two young children, she, godmother to one of them, went to the Old Vic, and was a Shakespeare enthusiast. A frequent visitor, she was overjoyed by my removal to such a convenient location, and under her guidance I soon became a devotee. Whenever the came to stay, we went to a play. In those days tickets were like gold; if they were to be obtained, plans had to be made well in advance, but we were young and overcame the difficulties. In the next five years we saw most of the great productions that were staged, and the Oliviers' *Macbeth* at last revealed to me what I had not understood before, despite my honours when examined on the play: the power of insomnia to dictate events. We saw *Titus Andronicus*, during which many in the audience fainted at the horrors – but not us. Would they faint today, when senses have been dulled by continual exposure to real and faked violence on film and television? Do audiences still find the putting out of Gloucester's eyes almost unbearable? I do – but I know the story and the sorrows that will follow, and that I will weep over the death of Cordelia. If I don't, it hasn't worked, and it always has: a shiver of anguish must echo the cry of 'Howl, howl, howl', and the lament of a bereaved heart-broken father who has brought about the killing of his daughter. I saw Robert Stephens – whom, with my cousin, I had first seen in *The Royal Hunt of the Sun* – in his great and grand finale, this time with a grandson who will, I hope, remember the experience.

My cousin and I saw Michael Redgrave as Richard II; she had survived exposure to the play at school and discovered the music of its language. I was already an aspiring writer and in love with words, and the poetry enraptured me. At that time I knew few of the plays themselves, and seldom read them in advance, but it was not necessary; before one's eyes the drama was disclosed as the writer had intended, and so good were the various productions in those years that the meaning was made clear even when the language was, occasionally, obscure.

I felt privileged to have seen so many great actors and

actresses in some of their finest roles. I saw Peggy Ashcroft's Portia but not her Juliet; however, I saw Dorothy Tutin and Judi Dench play Juliet, Viola and Portia. The productions and performances in those years set my standards. On the most fundamental level, they were not only dramatically memorable but also always audible, and convincingly costumed. I am a traditionalist, uneasy with gimmicks, but trickery – as in Adrian Noble's *Dream* and in Peter Brook's, is fine.

In 1955 I left the area, but an element of choice influenced my destination and I was eventually able to live, as I do still, about fifty miles from Stratford, an easy drive; recently the journey by car has been made even swifter, though less picturesque, by the M40 link. After the move, my cousin continued to visit and we went to the theatre more often than before. I began taking my children to matinées, carefully choosing which play we should see. We parked easily outside the theatre and picnicked in the Bancroft Gardens. Once I made a muddle, and brought my son and a friend to, as we thought, *Macbeth*, but it was *Cymbeline*. They loved it and forgave me, though it was many years before my son managed to see a performance of *Macbeth*.

It is difficult to imagine how different things would have been if I had not spent those years living so close to Stratford, with my cousin to lead me into the paths of right appreciation. Each play we saw, maybe for the third or fourth time in different productions, gave us something new to take away, even when it compared unfavourably with earlier productions we had seen. The only time this failed was, sadly, the last play we saw together shortly before her early death and that was Terry Hands's production of *Richard III* in 1970. We walked back to the car dejectedly, unable to find anything good to say about it because we felt the dramatist – and the cast – had been betrayed by the direction. Helen Mirren was Lady Anne in that production, and Ben Kingsley was Ratcliffe, Norman Rodway was Richard.

Looking through old cast lists – I have kept most of them since 1970 – it is interesting to see who played small parts then and are now distinguished actors, and others who showed promise but sank without apparent trace. In those days performances were balanced; stars shone, but they did not overshadow the excellent playing in smaller parts. This is not always true today; less experienced actors and those used to television can be inaudible even to theatregoers sitting near the stage. In leading roles, their inadequacies may be exposed by older actors now playing statesmen, lords and ladies, dukes and duchesses, who give proper weight to the words they speak and need employ no histrionics to create effect. Often the verse is lost. Today, certain directors seek to shock, to find new and controversial viewpoints, warping the focus of the play. Sometimes directional stunts distract from what is going on. When Kenneth Branagh first played Henry V, in a year of drought, the production included genuine rain before Agincourt, and, in about row G or so of the stalls, I was close enough to see at least one actor had positioned himself just within the range of the cascade and was getting wet; trivial speculation about how the water was circulated when everyone was being asked to save it entered my mind; was it being pumped in and out of the river in some way? In that same play we are asked by the dramatist to 'eke out our imperfections with your thoughts and think, when we talk of horses, that you see them printing their proud hoofs in the receiving earth'. Sometimes, today we are not allowed to deck our thoughts with kings; too many jarring or anachronistic strokes are administered – *The Merchant of Venice* set in a contemporary city office with men – and women – in suits. I avoided this production. Two young women, both actresses, approved of *Romeo and Juliet* in a version, which I saw with them, with Mercutio – or was it Tybalt? – driving a small red car. Of course it was amusing, as it is when real ponies appear in *Cinderella*, and if this experience led anyone to want more Shakespeare that has to be good, but where was the romance, the passion? *Romeo and Juliet* must be set close to its period or the prohibitions and conventions of the time make no sense.

The 1995 production was redeemed by a group of senior actors – the Capulets and Montagues, and Friar Lawrence – all of whom could hold the stage: they had presence, and not every younger actor has it. Preparing this piece, I asked my grandson, now aged thirteen, who saw the play, if he had felt there was a strong passion between the lovers and he had not; he had been more impressed by our backstage visit afterwards. He also saw, but not with me, the 1996 *Macbeth*, a play he had read at school, and his verdict was that it was not as good as the other Shakespeare plays he had seen; he prefers comedies to histories and tragedies and at his age, that is fair enough, but he shows discernment, too. After reading the reviews of critics whom I trust, I stayed away from the production of the Scottish play because I knew I would not like it. Formerly, I came up to almost everything; now I am very selective. Will there be another cycle of the histories, such as I have seen – *The Wars of the Roses*, Peter Hall's magnificent marathon in 1963 and *The Plantagenets*, directed by Adrian Noble, which I saw in London at the Barbican in 1989? Seeing all three plays on the same day was a marvellous experience. Memorable, too, were *Henry IV* and *Henry V* in 1966. Nearly thirty years later my two elder grandsons enjoyed *Henry IV, Part 1*, with Robert Stephens as Falstaff. Earlier that season, I had seen both parts in a single day, and had resolved to take them. I have tried to expose them to plays produced, according to reviews and following certain directors, in a reliable fashion, and I made two trips to *Twelfth Night* in 1994 so that my four grandchildren could see that good production, forming a yardstick for them. None of them, however, felt pity for Malvolio, who had been wonderfully funny. One should want to weep for him and for all the victims of cruel conduct and injustice – for Shylock being taunted, for poor Hermione with her jealous husband Leontes, and for Macduff – What, all my pretty chickens and their dam at one fell swoop? – and Macduff pulls his hat upon his brow.

I saw Vanessa Redgrave's Rosalind, but sometimes Celia has been taller than her cousin, making a nonsense of the distinction when she is described as being low, browner than her brother. Such casting – however good the acting – destroys illusion.

In the 1960s there was a sweeping change when, under Peter Hall's magnificent directorship, the Shakespeare Memorial Theatre became The Royal Shakespeare Theatre, with its own company, and began playing not only in Stratford but also in London at the Aldwych, where its range broadened to embrace classical and modern drama. With the creation of The Other Place in Stratford, and later the restoration of The Swan, this policy has expanded and now, in any season, a variety of theatrical experiences are available to the playgoer. Small companies travelled around the country, playing in schools and halls, with productions which had begun in The Other Place using few props and little staging, and since as early as 1913 major productions have toured the world. Most recently *The Winter's Tale*, in a romantic and exciting interpretation, musically embellished, demonstrated the excellence of British theatre internationally and, incidentally, earned foreign currency.

Nicholas Nickleby was tremendous, and may even have persuaded some who saw it to give Dickens a whirl. There have been other notable productions: *Les Misérables* began at the Barbican Theatre, which was designed and built for the Royal Shakespeare Company.

In 1990 there was a superb production of *The Seagull* at The Swan, with the wonderful, much lamented Susan Fleetwood – another great Rosalind – as Arkadina, and Simon Russell Beale, a fine and versatile actor, as a heart-rending Konstantin. The Swan lends itself to Chekov: a few trees or bits of furniture set the claustrophobic scene; intimacy with the audience is soon established. This extension of the range has to be of benefit to players and playgoers alike, but in Stratford, Shakespeare must remain central for he is the town's *raison d'être*.

The original Other Place was always great fun, and so is its more substantial successor, a good theatre to visit with one's younger friends. It is notable for its delight in using dry ice; mist and fog swirl around the actors at the slightest opportunity. The mechanics of acting are visible, often fascinatingly so, and sometimes the audience can take part, becoming members of the crowd in *Julius Caesar*, for example. The Trevor Nunn production in the earlier theatre of *Othello* was so immediate that one felt almost an intruder in the fatal bedroom as poor faithful Desdemona was so cruelly done to death. The destructive power of jealousy has never been better demonstrated than by Shakespeare in this play.

Music has played an increasingly strong part in productions, and some of the plays, such as *The Comedy of Errors*, have become musicals. There is room for change and innovation, even cutting, as long as the play retains its integrity. I took two boys to a matinée of *The Tempest*. After a hearty lunch, one drowsed off during Prospero's lengthy exposition of the past story, though his younger brother watched and listened raptly. I did not disturb the sleeper, who awoke to enjoy the part that really mattered: the unfolding tale of mystery and betrayal, and Prospero's farewell to his magic.

Times change, and so do our perceptions. We – and particularly the young – are used to a fast pace of life, to instant effects on film and television. The novelist must hook the reader on page one; similarly, the play must intrigue from its first moments, but this can happen if they are passed in silence as the actors take their places. Effects can emphasise the drama, but not if they distract by being introduced for their own sake, as all too often happens in the interpretations of some modern directors who seem to be saying, with Peter Pan, Oh, the cleverness of me. They do no service to the playwright, the performers, or the public. Excessive dissection of the text, which put me off in my youth, may have some effect on modern audiences when the eternal truths of Shakespeare's insight and the poetry are lost. Older playgoers bring their own prejudices and their knowledge to the theatre; we have seen the plays before, perhaps many times, and must remember that some of the audience may be perched on the edge of their seats wondering what will happen. Will Friar Lawrence's letter reach Romeo in time? Will Lear see the error of his ways? Can Macbeth's murdering rampage be halted? Will Hamlet's father be avenged? They must be allowed the chance to be entranced and spellbound, and honest interpretation is their right, otherwise they will not want to carry on the torch, as I have tried to do by taking young people and a variety of other friends, particularly those from overseas, to the theatre of Shakespeare in Stratford.

A new pleasure is the appearance of the sons and daughters of players well known in the theatre generally. They have to meet not only the challenge of the Stratford stage but of our expectations. Some of these débuts have been exciting.

All the logistical aspects of theatregoing anywhere, which were once so easy, are more difficult these days, even in Stratford, where now audiences for three theatres have to be accommodated. Parking can be a problem, though there is provision if you know where to find it, but there are plenty of places to eat, including excellent facilities at the theatre. Our evening routine is The Dirty Duck, which sets the scene and is so near, but lately I have come up several times by coach with a group organised by two theatre loving teachers, and we bring sandwiches because we may not arrive in time for anything more esoteric. With them, I have sometimes seen plays which I would not have made the effort to go to on my own, and having failed to get tickets for *The Cherry Orchard* in 1995 because it was sold out, I saw it with them in 1996; our organisers had planned well ahead. They take us by coach to The National Theatre, too, and to The Barbican, which I can never find if I attempt to drive there.

Stratford and the Royal Shakespeare Theatre have been important to me not only for the enrichment of learning to love the plays. After publishing eleven straight novels which were popular in libraries but not lucrative, I turned, like many another needing money, to crime, but in my case by proxy, inventing an amateur sleuth, Dr. Patrick Grant. Of course he had to have a job or profession with which I could empathise, and as I had worked in two Oxford college libraries, he was an Oxford don and a Shakespeare scholar in whose learned wake I trailed: he an expert, I merely an enthusiast. He featured in only five novels, but Shakespeare came into all of them, and in the last one, *Cast For Death*, a production of *Macbeth*, staged in a small fictional London theatre, played a crucial part. I would not have created Patrick Grant, whose appearance resembled that of Gregory Peck in *To Kill a Mockingbird*, if I had not lived near Stratford and seen all those wonderful productions where the plays and their eternal verities were treated with respect. Ultimately, I might have discovered the true, immortal Shakespeare; probably I would have done so; but the effect might not have been as profound.

I wonder what impact some recent productions – say, *Richard III* in 1995 – would have on a fledgeling playgoer? That fine actor, David Troughton, whose performance as Bottom playing Pyramus was the funniest I have ever seen, was obliged to portray no one remotely regal but a jester wearing motley: not a villain, nor even a conniving schemer. Shakespeare himself was not too accurate an historian, we know, but such a travesty of presentation gives a totally false view of history; there should be a sense of period as was demonstrated in the fine historical trilogies. This was maintained magnificently with *Henry IV*, and is particularly important in an age when tradition is shown scant reverence and the young lack knowledge and perspective about their past.

The play's the thing. Directors should have these words engraved on their hearts.

INTERLUDE

The First Night of *Richard III*

ANTONY SHER

THE OPENING NIGHT. 6 p.m. Cold shower. Muttering 'Now is the winter.'

6.15 p.m. Mac arrives, relaxed and chatty, bearing piles of cards from downstairs. The heat of the evening is intense. As he advances with the hump I say, 'I don't think I can bear wearing that tonight, Mac.' He says, 'Righto mate, I'll go and tell them Richard's got better'. Phone rings. Bill, sounding stiff and formal; 'Just want to say have a good one.'

6.40 p.m. Fight rehearsal in the Conference Hall. The tension backstage relatively low. 'Good luck, good luck' is the constant greeting as people pass one another. Some of my cartoons have been opened and are being passed round, making people laugh.

6.45 p.m. Dressing-room. 'Give me ten minutes alone, Mac.' Strolling around doing 'Now is the winter.' Oddly calm.

6.55 p.m. Beginners' call over the tannoy. Look at myself in the mirror and say aloud, 'Right, let's go and play Richard the Third.'

6.58 p.m. Waiting in the wings with Allam, Paul Gregory, Jonathan Scott-Taylor and Guy Fithen. We peer at the audience through the tracery walls of the set.

'Come on you buggers, get into your seats.'

'Look, the critics are writing already.'

'Tony, when your crutches first appear expect a cacophony of scribbling.'

7 p.m. Graham Sawyer arrives from front-of-house to give the final clearance. Philip mutters into his mouthpiece 'Going' and the house lights start to dim. The music crashes and I scurry on stage. Get into position and feel the lights change. Open my eyes.

'Now is the winter ...'

The first thing that strikes me is that the audience might be in more of a state than I am. Waves of tension that you can reach out and touch. How stupid first nights are! The frosty passivity of the critics ('We're not actually here, we're just observing') mixed with the nervous supportiveness of friends, relations and theatre staff. It's like playing to a dozen audiences at once. The laughter is muted and only starts about a third of the way back, behind the scribbling heads. A feeling that there might be some real people, ordinary members of the public, out there somewhere.

I underplay moments, overplay others, in an attempt to reach this totally untypical jumble of spectators. I dry briefly in

84

the Lady Anne scene and have to do one of my Shakespearean rewrites. Later in the same scene I'm horrified to hear my line 'I'll have her' come out as 'Oil'av'er!' Still, there is an exit round, albeit rather token.

Better from here on in. Realizing that I'm expending too much energy in trying to sort this lot out, I calm down to the point of indifference. Whenever I go backstage, worried faces loom out of the dark to whisper, 'How's it going?' 'Extremely well,' I keep replying and take a perverse delight in their expressions of surprise. Know what they're thinking, 'Well, he's not getting the laughs he got at the previews.'

At the coronation the big moment comes – Mal comes to disrobe me. We share a smile and I whisper 'Your big chance, Mal, go for the money.'

Don't know whether he managed it or not. Forget to ask afterwards.

The second half is much better. The audience appears to have decided it's not at all bad. They're more relaxed and confident and therefore so am I. Who's in charge here?

My voice lasts well, and, thank God, I've got some big guns left for oration. But no breakthrough on the nightmare speech.

Curtain call. The applause is disappointing, but I'm told there were some bravos and we are called back for another one. Blessed, Mal and I yell to one another over the applause, 'Well, you're on yer holidays!' Glimpse the scribblers scurrying up the aisles, dashing to their deadlines. Wonder how they find enough telephones?

Great relief backstage. People surround me, hugging and patting, Blessed sweetly saying, ''Kin marvellous performance, inspiration to us all, great triumph.'

In the dressing room, a race to get out of the drenched deformity and into the shower before people start arriving.

Standing naked under a stream of water, shampoo, soap, stage blood, running mascara – the most beautiful feeling. I survived.

A knock on the door and, through the rushing water, a familiar hoarse voice: 'Tone, where are yer?' Gambon!

Lots of other faces from the old Company: Chris Hunter, Monica McCabe, Ludo Keston, Dusty Hughes. How wonderful that they should have come all this way.

Now the dressing room full of RSC hierarchy. Suddenly Trevor Nunn pushes his way through and 'Trevs' me. I've heard a lot about this 'Trevving', but never had it done to me. From what I'd heard, a 'Trev' is an arm round your shoulder and a sideways squeeze. But this 'Trev' is a full frontal hug, so complete and so intimate that the dressing-room instantly clears, as if by suction. I'm left alone in the arms of this famous man wondering whether it's polite to let go.

He says, 'When this show moves to London there are going to be queues round the block. It's going to be one of those.'

A flash of a night in Joe Allen's some millennia ago.

At last alone. Step outside on to the little balcony, gasp at the fresh air. The storm never happened. It's a gloriously warm, almost Mediterranean night.

At the Duck, Pam whispers that the word is good and nods towards a table where they sit: Billlington, Coveney, Tinker and others. These crazy evenings in the Duck after an opening night, when we all pretend we don't know one another – us and them. I miss James Fenton because he used to cross no man's land and offer you a drink.

Mal and I sit with Gambon and his companion, Lynne. Try

and recapture the patter of two years ago, but there is something melancholy in the air. Beginning the descent. Gambon starts to talk about how strange it was driving into Stratford tonight, and his eyes fill.

We go to the party. It has been arranged by Steve, Jonathan, Guy and Hep. They have floodlit the garden of their digs. There is a barbecue and a *Richard III* cake to cut. Something which has happened, invisibly, over the last couple of weeks is that the Company has cemented together round this show. The cynicism and indifference are gone. There is a new enthusiasm for the work. I think that's one of this production's triumphs.

The only wet blanket this evening seems to be me, sitting alone at the back of the garden, forcing myself to eat although I still have no appetite. The exhaustion is massive, preventing me from having even one wild night of celebration.

Eventually find Bill. He has slumped alone in the living-room. Looking as wrecked as I feel. We smile at one another. Nothing left to say.

Later, I'm glad to have the opportunity to tell Gambon that at last I understand why he felt so disparaging about his great performance as Lear. At the time his behaviour seemed like destructive modesty. But Shakespeare's great parts are humiliating to play, or at least, humbling. You get to meet his genius face to face.

Leave the party early. Have to do it all again tomorrow and then again on Thursday.

Walking through Stratford on this warm, clear night. Not a soul about, just the beautiful timbered buildings, which often you can't see for the crowds. Late at night this place looks like any quiet country town.

Jim and Lynne fall behind as Gambon and I stroll along Waterside saying very little. It means a great deal to me to have him here tonight. Lear and Fool. Where this chapter of my life began.

BEHIND THE SCENES

Speaking the Speech

CICELY BERRY

I make notes on every workshop that I do, and looking back over the time I have been with the RSC has made me look through all those notebooks, to try and find what my priorities were 25 years ago, and see the ways in which they may have altered. It also seemed very likely that this would reveal something interesting about the audience expectations of the time. So this is a retrospective in terms of the voice work which has developed in the company which may give some sense of the changes that have taken place regarding the speaking of the text.

My first entry for the Summer School was I think in 1975, and the heading I gave myself for the workshop, i.e. my point of entry for the session, was:

'When speaking Shakespeare text the actor walks a continual tightrope between the formal and the informal.' – Peter Brook.

Now this is a rough quote for I do not remember Peter's exact words, but that premise I suppose has stuck with me ever since I first worked with him on *A Midsummer Night's Dream*. My intention with the group therefore was to illustrate this practically by working on a piece of text in order to discover how the language moved between the naturalistic and the heightened mode. And I think this question has been at the centre of my work ever since.

For the question is this: how does the modern actor feel truthful speaking classical language now? How does he/she honour the rhythms, the word games, the often extravagant imagery which is written there in the text and which is integral to the meaning, yet make it speak/sound for now? For that is what is important, that it sounds truthful to our ears now – that is what the actor is ever striving for.

I will come back to this question later: but first I would like to put the Voice work in context with the Company work – and this means of course how it fuses with the work and the views of the directors. We will begin to see just how complex this issue is: i.e. how we, as individuals, hear the spoken word.

In 1969 Trevor Nunn asked me to join the Company to work with the actors on Voice. To begin with I only worked part-time, but the work quickly grew and it soon became full-time, and this showed the importance Trevor placed on the language skills of the Company: it was the first Company to employ a Voice person on a full-time basis. By the way, the term is now Voice Coach – but I prefer Voice person!

My brief was to work with the actors on Voice: i.e. to make sure that everyone could be heard easily and clearly in the space – there was only one space then, the Main House. In other words I was responsible for all the Voice Production, with all that term implies – plenty of breath, clear diction, good range and no strain. This fitted in with my background of teaching young actors at the Central School, and with a great deal of work with professional actors.

However, my real interest, passion you could call it, had always been with poetry and how we speak it aloud – the subtlety of rhythm and cadence etc., and how all these textures/nuances of rhythm need to be heard for us to understand the text fully: and implicit in this is the question – how do we hear it? So, working with the Company enabled me to focus on this whole area by helping each actor to find both the voice and the language, and, most important, their own freedom of imagination within it. And each actor works and responds to text differently.

I was particularly lucky in that at the beginning I was working mainly with three directors – Trevor Nunn, John Barton and Terry Hands – all of whom had very different approaches to acting styles, and inevitably to the speaking of text: this really opened my ears, for their different styles necessitated different approaches to how the actors spoke.

This was something that I had not engaged with before. Up until now I had thought that the speaking of text was something which was totally to do with the choices the actor was making for him/herself in relation to character and motive. But now I began to realise to what extent the concept/style of the director influences the way the actor speaks on stage. And each of these three directors had quite different views on how the text should be spoken.

To put it very broadly: in rehearsal Trevor Nunn concentrated very much on the interaction between characters, their motives and emotional needs. This resulted in an informal and intimate style of speaking: my job therefore was to work with the actor to keep that initial response, yet make it big enough for the space – mostly the Main House – and encourage the awareness of the heightened language values within the less formal speaking style – in other words to find both its public and private sound. His famous production of *The Winter's Tale* with Judi Dench was a wonderful example of how the personal and the heightened language could fuse.

John Barton took what appeared to the actors to be a more academic line. His focus was on the specifics of the imagery, plus he was meticulous about the shaping and structure of a speech and the way the iambic pentameter worked – for that gives it the drive-through of the thought.

He was never dictatorial about this, but young actors very often felt inhibited: and so my job in his rehearsal process was to try to find ways to get the actor to respond freely to the character yet within the parameters that John had set. He did allow great freedom for the actor in the end, and his production of *Othello* still lives in my ears.

The challenge from Terry Hands often seemed formidable in that he wanted the actor to get speed through the lines, and he also wanted clarity with that speed – louder and faster was the battle cry! Actors who had not worked with him before found this difficult in that they felt they were not being given sufficient time to feel their way through the text and experiment with the meaning before they got the speed he demanded: this resulted often in a lack of texture. My job here was to take the actors away and work in detail on the speech – i.e. the changes of thought and how the thought moved in different rhythms through the speeches: they needed to find their own vocal variety within the speed Terry asked for. It proved to be a great learning process for me, for though I felt antagonistic to his method at first, I began to see the value of getting actors to think more quickly – Shakespeare needs to be spoken at the speed of thought. I remembered when Terry directed the three parts of *Henry VI* which went at a great lick the speaking started out to be level and rhythmically monotonous, but with the familiarity that they acquired by playing through the season the speaking became so much richer and more textured that, by the end of the run, it was like a long poem and wonderful to listen to. It had speed, variety and excitement. But this takes a huge amount of skill – something only acquired by practice.

Each of these three directors had a very clear idea of how they wanted the text to be spoken – how they wanted it to sound. And this of course was invaluable to me in that it made me very sensitive to the needs of the actor, and also very aware of the possibilities of the text. For the director working on Shakespeare a taste in the spoken word is essential: I believe how the actor uses the text can be as exciting and vivid as the setting. Again to quote Peter Brook – 'the language should be as exciting as dance'.

Now what this initial period in the Company did for me was (a) to make me realise the infinite number of ways a line of text can be spoken – Peter used to say that there were a million ways of saying just one line: and (b) to make me find ways to help the actor inhabit the text for him/herself whilst fulfilling the demands of the style which the director has set. And so I developed ways of working on text to make this happen.

You will gather from the number of references that I have made to Peter Brook that he was the person who initially inspired me: he conceives language as being integral to the whole movement of a character, and his work on the text of *A Midsummer Night's Dream* was inspiring – the language was both joyous and immediate – on the word. Without the word the action would not have happened.

I was also lucky in that soon after I joined the RSC Maurice Daniels started a strong education initiative, organising actors to go into schools and do practical workshops with the students. These were the humble beginnings of what is now our highly efficient and structured Education Unit. What I learned from these workshops was invaluable in that it made me find ways which combined the speaking of text and physical movement, often quite strenuous, so that the actors felt for themselves the physical action of the language: and I found that it helped them to understand the underlying meaning of the text more quickly. In other words, it made the text active for them, and made them experience what words do to you when you speak them – and this greatly influenced my work with actors.

I have talked in detail about my interaction with the directors because I think it illustrates some of the complexity that an actor is faced with when acting Shakespeare, or indeed any highly shaped language be it classical or modern: for there is something in the very form and cadence of any piece of good writing which takes us into that other world – the world of the play. Yet we all hear language differently: we all have different expectations – we all have what I call 'that secret voice'.

And of course our ears are influenced by what we hear around us every day, and this in turn is influenced by television and the media – a sort of globalisation of the spoken word. Thirty years ago an actor could unashamedly work on the music of Shakespeare, on the rhetoric, but now this would not feel quite real. The actor has somehow to bring together a sound which is of now, without damaging the very physical cost of the language: for it is through this very physicality that we are put in touch with the anger/pain/joy which is there to be heard and experienced.

I did an experiment once in a workshop at The Other Place: I called the workshop 'Our Changing Language' and the experiment was on *King Lear*. We took a section of the scene in Act II. Sc.iv between Lear, Goneril and Regan when they are bargaining with him as to how many followers each will allow him to keep. The actors first played the scene in as near Elizabethan as they could muster: we then played a recording of it which was made about 20 years ago: we next played it ourselves as if it were a sitcom, and lastly we played it as we had evolved it in the production that I had directed.

The Elizabethan version was fascinating because although it was quite rhetorical in style, the actual sound of the language, with the long vowels and the sounding of the final 'r' sounds, was very physical and made it sound strong and down to earth: it freed it from today's RP – Received Pronunciation – with its middle/upper class overtones. And this question of accent is very important: I am glad to say that our ears are becoming much more open to variations of accent than they were even twenty years ago – one good thing that has come out of television.

The recording we played of the scene made some twenty/ twenty-five years ago just did not sound real – it was very well pronounced but artificial to our ears. Our sitcom version made sense but was so naturalistic and thrown away that it had no significance – i.e. the words were not defined, were not found. And the last version, the one which the actors had worked on, I think honoured the sound of the language, its definition – and yet seemed spoken naturally.

And I think this sense of defining the language, defining the thought, is perhaps the key for the actor now, for it can bring together the modern 'Method' style of acting with the true defining of the word, thus taking on board the very size of the image. And this is the reason why I have developed exercises which involve some kind of physical effort – some kind of resistance, for it helps the actor to marry the need to speak the words with the physical cost of the language, and therefore to convey the size of the image and the magnitude of the thought.

Perhaps what has changed so radically in the last twenty-five years is this: when I started working with the Company the emphasis was on how the language sounded: it had to be truthful of course, but it was the rooting of the sound which was important. Now, the emphasis is on the intensity of communication, and how the words reach and affect us.

But though perhaps in the 80s the speaking of text became possibly over-naturalistic to fit with the growing media influence, I think now we are reacting to that: actors are very keen to work on the rhetoric in the language, and have become keenly aware of its music and how it connects with the bottom-line meaning of the text.

We have got to keep it like that: and we have to ask our new young directors to really listen for the excitement and passion in the language, to accept that language can arouse the listener. Language has the power to take us into the world of the play – let us depend more on the word and less on the setting.

A View from the (Stage) Management

DAVID BRIERLEY

When I was new there were scarcely two: The Shakespeare Memorial in Stratford and, just, the Aldwych in - London.

January 1961 was a lonely month. I arrived at the Shakespeare Memorial Theatre as the rawest recruit to assistant stage management when almost all my colleagues-to-be were in London opening theatre No. 2. Only company manager Alisoun was in Stratford, and she gave me the kindliest of welcomes and started me on a desperately needed learning process.

I'd never worked as a professional theatre employee before. There had been plenty of amateur acting (but no wish to be a professional performer); a great deal of work in Cambridge theatre (stage, company and business management, and much of it with John Barton, via whom had come the introduction to Stratford); and work on undergraduate productions at both the Arts Theatre in Cambridge and the Arts Theatre in London.

There had been teaching – at the Perse School in Cambridge

where English was taught to the first and second years in a small theatre called The Mummery; and at King's School Macclesfield where the school hall burned down three weeks after the start of term, leading to an exciting battle for possession of the dining hall and a most satisfying thrust stage production of *Twelfth Night*.

But Stratford was the first theatre job.

Because of the absence of the rest of the stage management team at The Aldwych, the earliest memories are of place rather than people, and the strongest of these is smell. Forget greasepaint and size. Every stage door in the world now reeks of fuel oil (hose connection point just outside) and herbal tobacco (Charlie the fireman just inside). And it's hard to squirt diesel into the car without vivid stage door flashback.

Stage management quarters were in the Conference Hall, the rehearsal room embraced by the semi-circular walls of the original 1879 auditorium, and now the Swan Theatre. Walk into the Swan, turn right, and you are in my first office. We ASMs shared the curving room on the side closest to the RSC Collection, and Stage Managers lived in a mirror-image room on the other side, each with an entrance from the Conference Hall and an exit to the great oak doors still at the back of the Swan drum. Above us was a balcony from which the rehearsal floor could be lit and observed.

With hierarchical unfairness, not only did Stage Managers have bigger desks and a view of the river, but ASMs also had to share their space with two gigantic gas cookers. These monsters were fired up only once a year, for the ceremonial lunch on Shakespeare's birthday, which was served not, as now, in a marquee on Avonbank Gardens, but in the Conference Hall. This annual invasion of our space caused much grumbling

among the stage management, too, at having to yield possession of the Conference Hall to the Summer School each year –
but these were unenlightened times when education was much
lower on the theatrical agenda.

Alisoun sent me to work in the ASM's office on cutting
scripts for the first two productions of the season. Cutting
scripts is one of the drearier stage management tasks. No matter how many editions of the Shakespeare texts are available to
directors, they will invariably wish to import readings from
other versions into the ones they select, and they will usually
want to make cuts in the chosen text too. These amendments
have all to be inserted in the texts (in pencil, of course: nothing
too definite) before rehearsals start – and given that texts have
to be prepared not only for the performers, but for all members of the production team, technical departments and others
too, there may be fifty to sixty scripts to be prepared for each
new production.

My yet-to-be-met colleagues had the impregnable excuse of
being elsewhere, so the job, together with an assortment of
other chores, was all mine.

This first Stratford season of the London era was to be the
last to be rehearsed entirely in Stratford. After that, most of the
rehearsals for the opening productions of each Stratford season were to take place in London. This allows companies to
include performers who, during Stratford rehearsal periods,
are still playing the final performances of previous London
seasons. The companies then move to Stratford just a couple
of days before the start of technical rehearsals. This is logisti-
cally efficient, but one certain loss, as the lives of subsequent
Stratford companies have evolved in London, has been of that
defining moment when a whole new company arrives fresh for

six weeks dedicated pre-opening rehearsal on Shakespeare's turf. Nothing has quite recreated that 1961 sense of instant new life.

In 1961, uniquely, it happened twice.

First of all, at the end of my isolated January, the return to Stratford of the rest of the 1961 stage management team, buzzing from the great London adventure, was like the home-coming of the Ranyevskys. You could smell the cherry blos-som in Charlie's tobacco smoke as they flooded onto the rehearsal stage that awaited them in the Conference Hall.

On closer inspection it was clear that their impact was quite disproportionate to their number, because besides Alisoun there were actually only three people and a dog: Ann, Don, Geoffrey and Ann's miniature poodle, Kirsty. Ann and Don were stage managers and Geoffrey and I were ASMs. Deputy stage managers hadn't been invented, so in various permuta-tions of three per production, stage managers managed, ASMs took charge of props, and the prompt scripts were compiled alternately by either stage managers or ASMs. With some help from another Jeffrey later in the season, the four of us were to cover all the six Shakespeare productions of 1961, together with *The Cherry Orchard* which was to open in Stratford at the end of the season before moving to The Aldwych.

Then, a couple of days later the actors arrived, and the entire theatre was energised all over again. This was curious because the SMT hadn't been dark during January. There was then a full-scale well-attended winter visitors' season in progress which was to run until March; but without its own company in residence the theatre had felt deserted, and only now was there a dawning understanding of what life in Stratford would really feel like. After four years in Cambridge and two years' teaching there was welcome recognition of a new collegiate community. For most people, all of life was encompassed by theatre, Duck and digs, the latter two being not a diversion from, but a structural extension of the former.

Nowadays the RSC owns or has access to some seventy or eighty bedsitters, flats and cottages which are available for the use of each season's company, but in 1961 most digs were still in private houses, in many of which landladies still provided bed, breakfast and evening meal at times best suited to actors. I lived with a Baby Belling to cook on in a bed-sitter at 33 Evesham Place owned by Mrs. Chapman, who was an usherette. Michael and Richard, two young actors in the company, had rooms there, too.

There were other, more famous communal quarters in Stratford. On the river at Tiddington there were flats and bed-sitters in Avoncliffe, a rambling house in part of which Peter Hall also lived, while downstream at the gothic former hotel, Avonside, there was a mixture of shabby staterooms and garrets which were mostly regarded as the domain of the production wardrobe. There was hot competition for the few spaces in the Malthouse in Southern Lane which the theatre owned, and for the Ferry House next door (whose owner, Sam Shakespeare, later left it to the RSC in his will); but the place really to be, even though it wasn't on the river, was 18 High Street (above what is now Waterstones), home of the theatre's singing teacher, Denne Gilkes, where she always gathered round her a fine mixture from junior stage management to leading performers.

And so Rehearsals started.

These days, cross-casting between concurrently rehearsing productions is kept to a minimum, but for *Much Ado About*

Nothing and *Hamlet* those who weren't cross-cast were in the minority. Ian Bannen (Hamlet) and Elizabeth Sellars (Gertrude) were out of *Much Ado*, and Christopher Plummer (Benedick) was not cast in *Hamlet*. But Geraldine McEwan had Beatrice and Ophelia, Noel Willman had Don Pedro and Claudius, Redmond Phillips had Leonato and Polonius, Newton Blick had Dogberry and the Gravedigger, Barry Warren had Claudio and Laertes, and most of the rest of the company were in both shows. Cross casting in the stage management meant that for *Much Ado* and *Hamlet* respectively Ann and Don were stage managers, Geoffrey was in charge of book and props, and I was assigned to props and book.

Competition for rehearsal priority between the directors was intense, and, then as now, it was the job of stage management to keep the peace. Time and space were both to be fought over. The Conference Hall was the only fully adequate rehearsal room in which the stage area could be marked out and the rehearsal scenery erected, so on any occasion when it was possible to schedule concurrent rehearsals there was always a loser in Dressing Room 16 (now the powerhouse of box office activities), the Circle Foyer, the Territorial Army Drill Hall or some other decreasingly satisfactory venue. Also to be scheduled were calls for dance, singing, fights, wardrobe, wigs, publicity interviews. All of this will be familiar to today's stage management, as will the rigorous regime of three-session days with continuous work through morning, afternoon and evening calls.

The job of stage management was completely enthralling. It was at the very hub of the life of the theatre. During rehearsals stage management were the civil service without which nothing worked. Performers and creative teams relied on them absolutely. Essential lines of communication ran direct from stage management to every corner of the operation. Think of a department and there there was a stage management link. Production office, property workshop, scenic workshop, paintshop, production wardrobe, maintenance wardrobe, wig department – stage management were the conduit for a constant stream of information passing between the creative team, the rehearsal floor and the creative departments. As the production prepared for the move from rehearsal floor to stage, stage management would provide vital preparatory and transitional information for the stage, props, electrical, sound and music departments. Stage management were important collaborators with the press office, and had to have a good working relationship with the box office; and during performances the stage manager was responsible for every element of the show, and with the house manager assumed ultimate responsibility in the name of the theatre for the quality of the performance and the welfare of the audience, artists and staffs. From stage management you could see into every corner of the organisation, but your activities remained rooted in the direct, rehearsal and performance, morning, noon and night working relationship with the artists.

I loved it.

Today's stage management would not, however, have felt especially familiar with the opening rhythm of the 1961 productions. On Saturday morning, in a blacked out and stage lit Conference Hall, all performers showed themselves to the director and designer in costume, wigs and make-up in a formal dress parade, sometimes doubling as a photo-call. Throughout Saturday night and a first Sunday (following a couple of Saturday performances for all productions after the opener) the technical staffs cleared the stage and started to fit up the new production. The fit-up would continue through Sunday, and the objective would be to have the company on stage by mid-afternoon to start a technical work-through on however much of the set had by that time been erected. This might continue until the early hours of Monday morning, when the performers would break, and the staffs might continue with a lighting session before starting to strike the set and to restore performance conditions for Monday evening. It was common for staffs and sometimes stage management to work for forty-eight hours or more at a stretch with only the briefest of breaks. But I can't remember ever making out a timesheet. Sunday was the only paid extra.

During the following week, normal performances of the repertoire would be given, at the end of which there would be another Saturday night strike and build, ready for the resumption on Sunday of the previous week's technical work-through, often running again into the small hours of Monday morning. First dress rehearsal was on Monday afternoon and evening and as much of the night as was needed, and into the interstices of this 72-hour Saturday to Monday period were fitted set-dressing, paint calls, lighting calls, music calls, and work on all the other technical issues to be resolved as actors and physical production finally met on stage. The second dress rehearsal started at 10.00 a.m on Tuesday morning, with curtain up on the press opening at 6.30 p.m.

Thus opened *Much Ado*, with Sundays three and four repeating the pattern, without break, for *Hamlet*. How very different from a conventional, later twentieth century, post-Health and Safety at Work Act technical/dress rehearsal period of at least Sunday to Wednesday, with a first preview on Thursday or

Friday, and then a run of performances up to a press opening the following week.

Stage management are astonishingly resilient, but even the most robust stand in need of periodic relief. In 1961 our therapy was 15 miles from Stratford, and upon the declaration of a Compton Wynyates condition we would find the means to ease ourselves away for an hour or two in the calm of that most beautiful and soothing of Elizabethan places.

So after *Hamlet*, Compton Wynates; and after Compton Wynyates, *Richard III*.

Christopher Plummer was Richard, Bill Gaskill and Jocelyn Herbert arrived to direct and design, and Dame Edith joined the company to play Queen Margaret and become adored by everybody. The Royal Court met the Grande Dame and struck an interesting balance.

Desmond Healey's *Much Ado* set had been a delicate standing structure; Leslie Hurry's *Hamlet* was heavy gothic with much flying, and Jocelyn's *Richard* was a flown, cylindrical turret upstage right on an otherwise open stage, with applied wire mesh in steel, copper and brass, the finishes of which were required to look like silk. I was on props again, and it was during a double rehearsal call when I was working at the Drill Hall that I received a summons back to the theatre, where Alisoun asked me if I would like to be stage manager of the next production, which was *As You Like It*. Would I not!

Richard remained to be done, however, before I got on with my own show, and it was not without incident. Wire mesh that looks like silk is still wire mesh, and there was constant snagging of people and costumes. There was a possibility that Christopher Plummer might not make the first night, so the earlier technical and dress rehearsals were undertaken by his understudy, Gordon Gostelow. The long on-stage rehearsals were particularly hard on the feet, and I found comfort during the technically quiet bits in lying on my back in the wings, with feet pointing up the rake and head down. With Christopher Plummer back in action for the final dress rehearsal, it was from this tuned-in but switched-off position that my ears construed an onstage scream as 'David!!' I leapt towards the stage yelling acquiescence, and was floored by Ann, who as the fully awake stage manager knew that my services were not required as Richard continued to let rip at his 'Lady' Anne. Later, in performance, Richmond, with blood dripping from a gash over his eye, fled offstage in terror from Richard's sword, and had to be prised by Ann from the flat to which he clung, and forced back on stage to allow the play to finish with the correct victors and vanquished. A turbulent King.

And so to *As You Like It* – only the fourth production of the season, but all my own. It was an idyllic rehearsal period and an idyllic production. Vanessa Redgrave arrived to play the definitive Rosalind, with Ian Bannen as Orlando and Max Adrian as Jaques. Michael Elliott directed, leading a group which included designer Richard Negri, movement specialist Litz Pisk, and composer George Hall – the team which was later to be at the heart of the foundation of Manchester's Royal Exchange Theatre. The set was a full-stage, steeply curving grassy bank topped by a gigantic cedar of Lebanon with vast horizontal boughs of solid foliage. The downstage bough floated through the proscenium arch, and the fire authorities required that it should automatically lower and retract itself from the path of the safety curtain whenever the curtain was dropped in. Fred Jenkins headed the scenic workshop, and came close to tears of frustration during the tenchical rehearsals as he (successfully) fine-tuned the device he had invented to perform this trick. The commitment and emotional input of RSC craftspeople matches all other contributions to its work.

I have surprisingly few detailed recollections of *As You Like It*: the broad, general pleasure of working in the production was so intense that it wiped out many of the smaller memories. About a year after the Stratford opening, *As You* became one of the first RSC productions to be recorded for television, and thirty-five years later I saw projected onto a cinema a speckled, striated black and white print with a hissing sound track. It wasn't even my cast, because there had been some replacements after the production left my hands. But it was still magical.

As You brought a new stage managerial pleasure too, and one denied to today's colleagues. In 1961 the stage manager personally plotted the throws and spreads of all the stage lighting, and thereafter, whenever a stage changeover had been completed, left whatever rehearsals he or she was engaged in, and personally directed the stage electricians in the refocussing and re-setting of all the lanterns and lighting effects for the next performance. That really was the ultimate seal of ownership.

Romeo and Juliet was my show out, so I missed direct involvement in such excitements as the loss of the Romeo and refusal of the revolve to shift a massive and unbalanced set (much call for Compton Wynyates). We had, however, by this time ceased to be Memorial and became, to our great surprise, Royal, and that made these things easier to live with. Instead, I began to prepare for the last Shakespeare of the season, *Othello*.

Sir John and Dame Peggy were to join us for this final fling, and Franco Zeffirelli was both director and designer. Franco was in evidence long before the point at which most previous

directors and designers had put in an appearance, and it soon
became apparent that this was to be the big one. Franco was an
opera and film man, and recognised no limits in the requirements of a repertoire, drama house. His style was prolific, pala-
tial naturalism. All Venice and Cyprus was here. I was in charge
of what must have been one of the longest props and furniture inventories in British theatre. Franco organised a trip to
Snowshill to study the tooling of leather on renaissance lug-
gage chests and much else. We thought fondly of Compton
Wynyates which was in the opposite direction.

The flow of infinitely detailed orders into the scenic workshop, the propshop and the wardrobe was ceaseless, and the
paintshop worked non-stop. Marble, tapestry, drapery, flights
of steps, piazzas and massive pillars, and pillars, and pillars. We
kept losing count of the pillars. There were too many to be
accommodated in the theatre between use, so we created a supplementary pillar dock in the paintshop on the opposite side of
Waterside.

As the dress rehearsal ground to an exhausted close an hour
before the press arrived, the stage was invaded from nowhere
by Lila di Nobili and a group of Franco's like-minded friends
who commandeered baked-bean tins full of paint, brushes,
size and textured wallpaper in a last, climactic orgy of decora-
tive zeal. The final, calming stage management announcement
to the company before curtain-up warned them not to stick to
the wet set. The first night intervals took three-quarters of an
hour each as the pillars were manhandled between paintshop,
scene dock, wings and stage by a supplementary pillar crew.
The next day they were allocated to special pillar disposal
duties.

That was the end of Shakespeare in Stratford for 1961, but

The Cherry Orchard was a superb coda, utterly delightful from beginning to end under the gentle masterly control of Michel St. Denis. Dame Peggy, Sir John, Dorothy Tutin, Judi Dench, Ian Holm, Patience Collier and Kirsty the poodle (promoted to performer after serious audition by Michel and Patience) were unbeatable.

After that it was The Aldwych with *The Cherry Orchard*, and the start of London rehearsals for the first two productions of the 1962 Stratford season. On Don's departure, I joined Ann as a full stage manager. When we got married it had to be on the last Friday of the 1962 season because that was when *The Taming of the Shrew* was playing – our show out – and on Saturday we had a get-out to attend to.

Later, I became company manager in London, Peter Hall's administrative assistant, and, in 1968, RSC General Manager. At each of these moves I gave serious thought to pulling rank and demanding that I be allowed to keep my hand in as a stage manager for, say, just one production a year. It wasn't, of course, a practical proposition, but it was a good dream wish, and it has been a lasting sadness that future activities led further and further away from the stage managerial front line.

The last time Ann and I went to Compton Wynyates there was no way in to the park and the house was visible only through a chained gate.

Don't put your daughter on the stage, Mrs. Worthington, but consider killing to get her into the Stratford stage management.

'Bit by bit, putting it together'

ROGER HOWELLS

Let me tell you something of the technical aspects of bring-ing a production to the stage, drawing on experiences in the Stratford theatres.

To those of us involved in the technical side, the beginning of the process which eventually leads to the physical present-ation on stage of the production is a meeting between the designer, often the director, and the representatives of the technical departments who are concerned with translating ideas into fabric, wood, metal, all sorts of synthetics, paint and light.

The designer and director bring to that meeting the product of discussions which have arrived at a visual concept of the play, which they will show as a design, almost always in the shape of a model.

The interested parties in-house who will want to see the set model include the heads of the scenic workshop, the property workshop and the paintshop, the scenic draftsman, the chief stage technician, the head of the property department, the chief stage electrician, the design assistant, the stage manager and the production manager. The lighting designer, who is frequently a freelance from outside the RST, will usually want to be present as well.

What sort of model are they all looking at? It will usually be made by the designer to fit inside a 1:25 scale model of the appropriate stage provided by the design assistant.

Surely everything is now clearcut and straightforward. All these skilful and talented people will simply study what is put in front of them and launch into the process of translating the model into a full-size version of itself. The designer will then meet the wardrobe department, show them the costume designs, and they too will get on with it. Everything will come together at the dress rehearsal.

The reality of the situation, where in Stratford alone we have three theatres, the RST Main House, The Swan and The Other Place, which will simultaneously be introducing new productions into their repertoires, is that our own workshops will frequently not be able to cope with the sheer volume of work. Outside independent contractors will then have to be involved in some capacity.

A broad decision might be made by the production controller that, say, the scenery for a Swan production cannot be dealt with at all by the RST scenic workshop because the competing Main House production will need its full resources. For the same production it might be decided that it is possible on the whole for the property workshop and the production wardrobe to cope with the show's demands. The process then assumes a slightly different pattern.

The involvement of an outside contractor cannot be ignored because it happens so often, but at this stage, before we even consider who does the work, we must ask the basic design question. Can it be done at all?

This is our first digression from the neat, direct narrative path, for an example readily comes to mind of one situation when an external firm was contracted, but only after that fundamental question had been answered.

Murder in the Cathedral was to be mounted in The Swan and the RST scenic workshop was completely tied up with other work. A model was produced within manageable time, although both director and designer had to work on their concept while still engaged on other projects, at least one of which involved spending time in America. The practicality briefing had taken place between the production manager and the designer when the model box was delivered. The budgetary limit had been passed on, plus information concerning the physical limitations of the building, the time limit on changeovers between matinée and evening shows, the shortage of storage space, the difficulty of access between stage and storage area and the limitation on the numbers of available staff.

After a genuine attempt to meet all the required criteria, the design which emerged was felt by the production manager not to meet the practical requirements. The classic design situation had arisen. If you reject a design and ask for a new one, will it be right next time? Even if it is, have you so reduced the time available for construction that you are forced to enter overtime and drive up the cost?

The inevitable next step was a meeting between director, designer and production manager, and fortunately it was possible to get all three together at short notice. The worst case would have been if someone had not been available for several days. The difficulties had to be gone over again and clear reasons given why the design was unacceptable. Compromises were offered along with practical suggestions for achieving an approximation to the design which would avoid the imposs-ibilities of handling and storage.

These were rejected by the director and designer, who felt that compromise was an unsatisfactory solution to the prob-lem, although they now saw that the original design was un-workable. They elected to provide a new, simpler design, which still preserved an acceptable artistic coherence, where com-promise would have produced a muddled image.

This is an unusual occurrence which proved, in the event, to be a satisfactory solution because a new design emerged within forty-eight hours.

So we were now ready to proceed to the next step. The designer had recently worked with a firm of contractors whose work he liked. We approached them and they were available. A series of meetings took place between them, the designer, the production manager and the chief stage technician of The Swan, who would be primarily concerned with the day-to-day handling of the set. Then additional specialist contractors were brought in to paint and manufacture a particular fabric element of the design. Costings were agreed upon and construction got under way.

Meetings with the head of the RST properties workshop looked at costs and allocated the manufacture of furniture and some smaller props within the department. It was agreed that certain items should be made by a local blacksmith and metal-worker. Metallic coatings would be carried out by a firm in the Midlands. We were now dealing with contractors in London, Cardiff, Elstree and Ledbury.

Costume designs submitted to the production wardrobe

were discussed and the making divided between our own teams and some freelance costume makers.

So much for the not untypical division of manufacturing skills in one Swan production.

The crucial thing to bear in mind is the interplay and individual input of creative skills from such a wide range of people. A designer may have a complete vision of a finished design and how it might be achieved. On the other hand the method of achievement and the materials to be employed might come from any one of a number of contributors. Give and take is an essential part of the process and of course all the elements must be co-ordinated and a continuing awareness of progress maintained across the whole range of activities.

To revert to a situation where the radical decision for an entire remake does not have to be made, let us go back to a Main House production and the first presentation when the designer and the director take us through the production scene by scene with the aid of the model.

It is a significant meeting. For most of the participants it is their first glimpse of the concept and the extent of their participation. First general impressions must give way to practical, concrete ideas. Many questions will need answers.

Who will do what? How does the work divide? Are there grey areas where it is uncertain what should be dealt with by the scenic and what by the property department? What about textures and finishes? What is the involvement of the paint-shop? Are there areas of work where an outside contractor should be considered? How does the design fit in to the context of a four or five play repertoire? How well can it be constructed to dismantle and store in the limited space in the theatre? How quickly, easily and safely can it be changed to and from the other plays in the repertoire? How robustly can it be made and yet, if necessary, retain the appearance of delicacy? What must be flown and by what methods? What additional machinery might be required? Do we need lifts or traps? What materials do we need? Can we use manual power or will we have to use electric motors or a hydraulic system? Do we need extra lighting equipment? How much money do I calculate is required to carry out my part of the overall task, and how much will I be allowed as my proportion of the whole budget figure? What sort of timetable do we allow for the various phases of the work?

At the end of the meeting there is much food for thought. Certainly more detailed and precise costing has to be arrived at and where big discrepancies occur between the perceived cost and the actual money available more negotiations will take place involving the workshop concerned, the production manager and the director's team. The process can sometimes continue for weeks.

Now rehearsals will be under way and the director will be less available for meetings, which will often take place in time snatched from meal breaks.

Rehearsals bring changes too. It is one of stage management's responsibilities to keep all parties informed of the new ideas that flow from the rehearsal room. Requests and suggestions from director and actors are written down and copies passed on regularly to the production departments. Each suggestion generates questions. Does this need following up, or is it likely to be discarded? If it is a serious idea, how much will it cost? Can the budget accommodate it? Can a particular object be bought off the shelf? Is it in stock? Has it to be specially made? If so, can we have a design? If we are cutting object X will it save enough money to pay for the alternative object Y? Is it too late because the money has already been spent on beginning its fabrication? If the set is particularly difficult for the actors to cope with physically, have we the time and money to supply a near-duplicate version in the rehearsal room?

The work proceeds, but questions are continually being asked and the juggling process goes on. Money is of the essence because there is a budget figure to be met. Time is of the essence because there is a fixed opening date when everything has to be brought together. Consequently great emphasis has to be put on the up-dating of information. Changes of all sorts have to be dealt with until the moment when everything, including lighting, music and sound comes together on stage, with the actors.

Of course some problems can be anticipated. When the model of *The Thebans* in The Swan was first shown, the stage floor was covered in a layer of loose material. When asked what it was, the designer requested something that resembled black volcanic ash. A question to the director elicited the expected answer that bare feet and limbs would be a fairly common feature of the production. Familiarity with the basic plank stage of The Swan told us that a fine hard granular substance would get between the floorboards and also spread all over the auditorium – and what would it do to bare limbs? The solution turned out to be black, fire-proof foam rubber used for car upholstery, chopped up into small pieces by an industrial shredder. It was still a difficult material to handle and store, but at least there was no abraded or torn flesh among the company.

Approximately six weeks after the first detailed showing of the model, the milestone of the fit-up or production weekend arrives. On the Sunday morning immediately before the first preview (which is usually on a Thursday) the elements of the set are delivered to the theatre from the RST's or the contractor's workshops. The stage crew strike the set of the previous night's performance, start getting-in the new show and fitting it up with the manufacturing carpenters from the workshops. Sometimes, if circumstances require and allow it, preliminary work will have taken place on stage the previous weekend. Everything will be done to make the stage ready for the company to begin technical rehearsals as soon as possible. Variable factors in preparing each new show mean that this can never be a fixed time, but usually the work schedule aims at getting the company on stage on the Monday evening or the Tuesday morning with the basic set in place, props to hand, lights positioned and focussed and the majority of costumes ready.

From the beginning of technical rehearsals to the time of the Dress Rehearsal (preferably on the Wednesday evening) there is a lot of work to fit in. Sometimes the first preview starts late because the Dress Rehearsal runs late on the Thursday afternoon. Sometimes there is no Dress Rehearsal, so the first preview is the Dress Rehearsal. This happened, for example, when Michael Bogdanov directed *The Taming of the Shrew* in 1978.

In these circumstances the practice of holding a series of previews before the Press Night, as opposed to the old practice of a First Night following the Dress Rehearsal, is extremely valuable.

The main function of the previews is to polish and fine tune the production, but few will deny that it can provide an opportunity to do more if a more radical change is needed. The ideal of course is that the technical rehearsal period and the Dress Rehearsal will solve all difficulties and provide a platform for a problem-free first preview.

From the time when the auditorium lights first dim for the technical rehearsals, all lighting cues, scenic changes, flying cues, prop moves, music and sound cues, effects, actors' entrances and quick changes must be rehearsed, co-ordinated and plotted so that they can be repeated precisely under the supervision and guidance of the stage management.

Through this final rehearsal period and beyond, during the days of the previews, alterations will continue. In snatched moments, when the company is not on stage, tidying up and improving the set and lighting will almost certainly be continuing, while painters will be painting and props and costumes will be whisked away to be altered and improved, or finished.

About this time, too, the production manager may well have already started pursuing the director and designer of the next production coming into the repertoire.

Is the end in sight therefore? Does the arrival of the Press Night mean that the current production can now be left to live its own life? There is a seductive satisfaction in leaving the Press Night behind and moving on to the challenges of the new production, for no two are ever alike, but once the show enters the repertoire, responsibility does not end. Maintenance is constant. Refurbishing, repairing, repainting and replacement will continue throughout the run, fitting in when required wherever possible in the daily routine of matinée and evening performances, changeovers and on-stage rehearsals.

All the foregoing is, in a sense, the routine pattern of work which one terms 'practical' because it deals with the planning and execution of 'hands-on' skills. On the whole it deals with foreseen circumstances, but frequently added satisfaction is found in coping with an unexpected occurrence.

Two instances occurred in 1969. At the end of a day's technical rehearsal for *The Winter's Tale*, in a basic 'White Box' setting which formed the background for the season's plays, the general thinking was that things had gone well and fairly smoothly. We had moved into Bohemia for the sheep-shearing festival and the dances had just been rehearsed so the company was released for the night.

However, Trevor Nunn, who was directing, was not happy with the sound the band was producing. He wanted a 'Big Band' sound. The RST Wind Band was used to playing on-stage in costumes, or in a variety of positions in the wings. On-stage was not an option in this case, as unamplified their numbers could not produce the effect required. In the wings they could be amplified but the acoustic would be variable as more shows joined the repertoire and differently stacked scenery and re-positioned musicians would continue to change conditions. Re-balancing the sound levels every time there was a changeover to *The Winter's Tale* from another play was not practical, particularly in those instances when there would be a clash with the unavoidably noisy activities of stage technical departments.

When the company came back the following morning to continue rehearsals we had to have achieved what Trevor needed. The solution was to allocate a specific space to one side of the stage and create a permanent area with an acceptable simple acoustic surround. The sounds from the various instrumental groups could be balanced and stay balanced, with minimal adjustment from time to time. After a brief postponement of the dance rehearsal in the morning to give the band time to adjust, we were back on course. The only other difficulty was ensuring that all future productions that season would fit into the remaining wing spaces and could not be allowed to encroach upon the hallowed 'band box'.

The significant development from that time was an acceptance that subsequently there should always be available a definite sound studio type of area. The following season the band box site was moved upstage to another position where it did not create so much pressure on the wing storage. At the same time it was possible to replace the old curtain surround with a properly built partition wall.

Eventually, in the 1980's a further improvement took place when the band was moved once again, to a more convenient and less claustrophobic area. Another space at the back of the stage had height which was seldom taken advantage of to house tall items. By building a strong platform the band could be provided with an upper room better than their previous area, while some storage and free passage-way could be preserved below at stage-floor level. And so an overnight quick solution to a problem led to the provision of a facility (good amplified music from a guaranteed studio type of space) which is now accepted as fundamental to the presentation of most productions.

A second instance at the end of the same season illustrates how the unexpected can wrong-foot one. *Henry VIII* was the last play into the White Box permanent set for the season. Everything else had gone rather well and we were probably feeling complacent. Again, at the end of the first day's technical rehearsals, Trevor and John Bury, who had designed *Henry VIII*, agreed that their set did not work satisfactorily inside a white surround. The white box would have to become a black box by the following morning. The change of concept was radical but the problem was not insurmountable. There was sufficient black serge available in the scenic workshop store to fix in position swiftly if temporarily. During the next few days of rehearsal, preview and performance there was time to have manufactured a set of masking drapes which could be attached and detached reasonably easily and quickly whenever we were required to change to and from *Henry VIII* through the remainder of the season.

Neither of these spur-of-the-moment demands was impossible to meet, but they illustrate how there is often very little time to introduce a new idea or alter an old one.

Even when there is advance notice of a problem it is important to move quickly. Theatre time is always in short supply. Here are two examples of design plans revealed before a season began which demonstrate how necessary it is to investigate and consult as soon as possible.

In 1976 John Napier and Chris Dyer devised a brilliant permanent staging structure, affectionately known as the wooden 'O', part of which provided on-stage audience seating. The implications were far-reaching. How would the licensing authorities accept members of the public in the stage area, and what extra safety standards would be required? The stage is normally separated from the audience by a fire curtain and self-closing fire doors. What about additional fire exits, signs and access? What extra staffing would be required to look after the stage audience and protect them from back-stage hazards? The detailed questions raised covered many pages, and early answers were required before we could commit ourselves to major construction.

Not for the first time we were fortunate in obtaining a sympathetic and constructive response when we convened a meeting with representatives of the Licensing Authorities and the Fire Service to confront the problems and find practical answers. Suggestions and solutions were offered and accepted and the work went forward without unnecessary delay.

In 1984 the overall design plan for the season included a proscenium stripped back to the bare brick with the forestage taken across the full width of the auditorium and the doors on each side of the proscenium fully exposed. Until this time the door in the stage left wall had always been screened from view, allowing its use as a pass door on to the stage from front-of-house and certain dressing rooms. To expose it meant that there was no access from one area to the other during performance. The only way would be outside the building, along a terrace and in through the stage door. As this was an unacceptable situation it was clear that there had to be an alternative. By careful investigation we were able to identify the one place where a new pass door could be cut through. Again we were able to go ahead with that crucial preparation in advance and avoid delay in building the season's actual productions.

Problems which occur suddenly when the season is already under way are always more critical, for an instant response is called for.

One Friday evening towards the end of a performance of one of the plays in the Roman season of 1972, a grinding noise was detected under the stage. An elaborate system of lifts, traps and tilts controlled by hydraulic rams had been installed at the beginning of the season to provide a variety of scenic permutations. Upon investigation it was found that a large main bearing near the centre of the system had cracked and could soon bring all stage movement to a halt, perhaps in mid-performance. Some frantic late-night telephoning took place. The engineer who had been in charge of the original installation was contacted at his home in Berkshire. He thought that he could trace a replacement to a supplier in Manchester who might be open on Saturday morning. He would confirm in the morning. We were lucky that the two performances scheduled for Saturday were a matinée of *Julius Caesar* and *The Comedy of Errors* in the evening. On Saturday morning the stage was set carefully and made safe at a fixed incline. The *Caesar* production called for fewer stage variations than *Coriolanus*, *Antony and Cleopatra* or *Titus Andronicus*. As many of the company as could be contacted were called in for rehearsal into a simplified version of the production, dispensing with the floor movements entirely.

By even more good fortune the set for *The Comedy of Errors* was independent of the arrangements for the Romans and merely sat at the centre of the stage within its own surround. The changeover and evening show should be straightforward. Given the amount of leeway it was possible to take a vehicle to Manchester, collect a new bearing from the supplier and deliver it back to Stratford before the end of the afternoon. On Sunday the new bearing was substituted for the old one and on Monday the repertoire returned to normal.

Finally I cannot resist re-telling the story of what became an extended response to a problem that arose in performance, but proved not to be capable of an immediate simple solution. I refer to the case of Richard III's crutches, which has been mentioned by Antony Sher in *Year of the King* and which took several months to resolve.

A strong element in the performance of Antony's Richard III in 1984 was the 'bottled spider' appearance provided by the character's crippled legs combined with long black hanging sleeves and (slightly anachronistic) elbow crutches. The sketch provided by the designer, William Dudley, suggested primitive crutches made from something resembling gnarled and twisted bog-oak. In rehearsal Antony used conventional modern alloy tubular crutches with which he was familiar, having two years previously depended on them while recovering from injury to an Achilles tendon.

The rehearsal crutches stood up to intensive hard use as a weapon, for athletic vaulting, or for the very emphatic expression of rage as they were violently smashed against the furniture. To capture the gnarled root-like look of the design and provide the strength which rehearsals showed would be necessary, the Property Shop had a pair of crutches made from steel. They were found to be too heavy and it was agreed that it would be more satisfactory to continue using a modern pair and disguise their modernity by dressing them with black leather and antiqued metallic bands. A number of spare sets were provided for emergencies.

Some time into the run, part of the way through performances, one of the crutches buckled and cracked. It was quickly replaced by one of the spares standing by in the wings, but confidence in their safety had collapsed with the crutch.

To guarantee that there would be no repetition in future was a tall order, yet it was clear that the treatment the crutches received in a very physical performance was causing metal fatigue and a safe alternative had to be found. To buy time we purchased a large number of new crutches and disguised them in their quasi-medieval trappings. We then imposed a strict rule that each pair would only be used for a very limited number of performances before being replaced.

We had already begun the search for the perfect model. Our first contact was with the Metallurgy Department at Birmingham University who suggested a particular strong metal tubing used in modern bicycle frames. We obtained some from the factory and made up a prototype. We also contacted and visited the factory in Wiltshire which manufactured crutches for the National Health Service and discussed the problem with them. They provided us with several pairs of strong crutches expressly made for Third World countries. Both types stood up well to mechanical testing in the University laboratory, but collapsed when tried out by Mr. Sher in rehearsal conditions.

It seemed sensible to follow a new course suggested almost casually by a member of the Metallurgy Department. 'Have you considered that metal tube might not be the appropriate material? Have you thought about wood?'

We thought about wood. The trail led to a furniture maker who had been an engineer with Rolls Royce and, coincidentally, while in the navy, a member of a quarter-staff team. He thought he understood the problem and came up with another prototype. History repeated itself. Laboratory testing was optimistic; Sher-testing found the breaking-point in short time.

Casting around for yet another approach brought in a freelance engineer who was also one of our regular weapon designer/makers. We talked around many ideas. Perhaps strength and rigidity were not enough. A vaulting pole had to have flexibility. Wasn't the Mosquito, the wartime plane, build around a laminated wooden frame? Would laminated wood provide the strength and flexibility we required? If there were no joints cut into the main shaft where the handle and elbow loop joined wouldn't that reduce stress areas? Why not clamp and glue the handle and elbow loop externally?

The work went ahead to produce yet another prototype and this time acceptance and success were achieved. When the company took *Richard III* up to Newcastle at the beginning of the next year it took the new crutches with it. Eventually we had about six or eight spare pairs of the final version made, but they all lasted through Newcastle, the Barbican season and an Australian tour and came back with no breakages.

Henry V and *The Merchant of Venice* were already running when *Richard III* joined them, and while the crutch conundrum kept on teasing us through to the end of the Stratford season, we were dealing with succeeding productions of *Hamlet* designed by Maria Bjornson and *Love's Labour's Lost* by Bob Crowley, each one with its own fascinating and different problems.

It is easy to be self-indulgently anecdotal about any aspect of working in the theatre. Every production will produce hundreds of stories. It is equally easy to cloud the shape of the work where so much overlapping of interests, responsibilities and input occurs. In an organization such as ours a clear picture is even more difficult for an outsider to discern. There are some differences in all productions and even differences between the theatres. The Stratford Main House, The Swan, The Other Place, the Barbican Theatre and The Pit vary not merely in physical size and shape, but in details of staffing structures, style and the methods by which the production finally arrives on stage.

Nevertheless there is a basic pattern to the work which all share and the best features are seen in the attitude and skills of the people who work in the RST, the individual and corporate input and a special sort of teamwork which, finally, brings everything together at the right time and in the right place.

We might all feel we can indulge in a little sigh of satisfaction. But we can't relax. It isn't really over yet, and anyway we've already started on the next one.

Looking Back, Looking Forward

TREVOR NUNN

It is ten years since I left the Royal Shakespeare Company, and during that time I have worked entirely as a free-lance. But now I am about to take on the job of running the National Theatre, as successor to Richard Eyre and inevitably people have asked me ' Why on earth?' Meaning, why would I want to take on the job of directing a huge national theatrical institution with everything that entails all over again? And in trying to answer, of course I look back to my time with the RSC and I see more clearly things about the company and about what I tried to do as Artistic Director.

Make no mistake, in many ways I was enjoying my freelance time and being a gun for hire, doing a wide variety of work, being the sole decision maker about when I worked and enjoying considerable periods of time with my young family, too. But ... I was missing something very much and it didn't take me long to identify what it was. I was missing an artistic community. I was missing collaborators. That was what I most valued and what I remember most fondly about my RSC years, and what I most emphatically did not want to go on missing.

The ensemble company was largely the invention of my predecessor Peter Hall, because although of course we celebrate the earlier years of the theatre at Stratford, and Anthony Quayle and Glen Byam Shaw, the RSC as it is now began with Peter: the idea of permanence and of continuity, the idea of complete dedication to principles that would be maintained and developed over the years was his invention, at least as far as theatre organization in this country is concerned. He had models from abroad, of course, – the Berliner Ensemble in Germany, the Théâtre Nationale Populaire and to some extent the Comédie Française: they were what led to his idea of a permanent or semi-permanent ensemble, of a house style, and of certain common principles of design and presentation. Above all, when applied to the RSC, they led to a shared approach to the Shakespeare texts, the language of Shakespeare and the speaking of the verse. When I took over, I inherited all of this very real coherence.

I also inherited some serious financial problems and a number of large questions about whether the organization as we then knew it could continue and I think I also inherited a reality that was less commendable than the theory. There was a very large group of associate artists, some of whom had not in fact worked for the company for a very long time. There was an ensemble, but some were more ensemble than others. Added to which this was a company with a very long tail in the shape of a dauntingly large number of people paid simply to walk on, without lines, as armies and crowds. I knew that my first contribution must be to rationalize the results of Peter Hall's thinking, once I had found my feet (and when you begin a job like that it really is a bit like floundering in deep water –

you're not at all sure that you aren't going to drown, you keep reaching down to try to find some firm ground, but eventually your feet do come to rest.)

I have always been what is known as a Leavisite – certainly I have always wanted to proceed in the way the critic F. R. Leavis described, which is, roughly, to say that of course there is a way of defining value, excellence and the way is to ask the question, 'This is so, isn't it?' and expect the reply 'Yes, but. . . .'

I felt that I was being asked by Peter Hall and his achievements with the RSC 'This is so, isn't it?' and I wanted to reply, 'Yes, but. . . .'

The 'but' was that his achievements did need to be rationalized in some areas and in others to be intensified. From the start, I picked up on the principle that Peter established of a group of Associate Directors. There was already a Directorate, of course, of Peter Hall himself, Michel Saint Denis and Peter Brook and historically that was extremely important. But it was not always a very practical construct simply in management terms, partly because of the very nature of their various personalities. They were extraordinarily representative figures – history makers and a tremendous amount of status was derived by the Company from their presence alone, even just from their names at the top of the notepaper. But they were outstanding individuals not committee men, and in my experience, relatively little detailed season-to-season decision making was done by them or derived from them as a triumvirate.

What I tried to do was to establish a genuine group of Associates. And the minute I did that I became conscious of the need for training above all things. If you have a genuine ensemble company that wants to renew itself on an annual basis then there must be a group of directors who have previously dedicated themselves to working with that company. If you do not have a committed directorate and things are done in an ad hoc way, you run into trouble. For example, people who arrive to direct a single play and who are outside the dedicated group, see no reason why they should have to limit themselves to the actors already in the company: they know lots of other actors they would like to work with and friends they would like to bring in from here and there. What happens next of course is that those who have committed themselves to the company see the parts that they wanted to play and should be playing going to outsiders, new people who have not made and would not make any lengthy commitment. At that point the whole thing begins to break down.

I believed that there had to be a core group of directors who helped to create the acting company and committed themselves to it and that the actors must understand from the beginning that they were committed to working with those directors.

I also felt that it was very important to have talents which were developing and burgeoning and not ones which were either at a standstill or in any danger of merely repeating themselves in the work they were presenting. That is why training became my watchword and in two principal areas.

Firstly I set about appointing what I called at the time Assistant Directors, although the title was slightly misleading because in most cases they were more senior and experienced in the profession than would normally be associated with that title; but they knew that in accepting the title they had the opportunity to graduate to a position in which they were making a very considerable contribution to the work of the company. There was a sort of journeyman-apprentice relationship between the existing Associate Directors and these Assistant

Directors. We had a great deal of excellent discussion, almost in a tutorial style, about how the younger directors were progressing, what kind of work it was felt they needed next, how they could fill in the gaps in their experience. It was that training which produced the generation of directors that included Howard Davies, Bill Alexander, Ron Daniels, John Caird, Barry Kyle and Adrian Noble, and which also produced Buzz Goodbody, the first Artistic Director of The Other Place, whose career was tragically cut short by her death in 1975.

It still seems to me quite certain that the body of work we did then had a real coherence which, precisely because of the training, was not accidental, it derived from discussion and there was a deliberate and identifiable house-style from season to season. That was what gave a cohesion to Peter's original scheme, although at the time I was very conscious that even more might have been attempted, and conscious too that towards the end of those years people were beginning to say it would have been better if the group of directors could have been refreshed and challenged by some of the great international directors like Peter Brook and Peter Stein coming in to work with the acting company more regularly.

I certainly did not want to turn the RSC into a 'Directors' Theatre' in the Russian or the European mould. To me the all-important things were the primacy of the text and the primacy of the actor.

Which brings me to the second absolutely vital area of training – that of the actors, and in this John Barton was supremely important. His work, side by side with that of the voice coach, Cicely Berry, was ground-breaking, not because it was new in itself but because of the extent to which it imbued all the work in both houses, large and small. Ad hoc approaches to the acting of Shakespeare and the speaking of the verse became a thing of the past at Stratford.

There were actually two identifiable streams to John Barton's teaching although he has always tried to make sure that they are complementary streams not conflicting ones and to be himself the bridge between them. On the one hand, I was drawn towards using his teaching to demonstrate the astonishing, naturalistic techniques that Shakespeare discovered progressively during his writing lifetime and which became more noticeable in the conditions of the small theatre, where the speaking of the text is at conversational level. In this situation, where the actor is not projected, the thought process, choice of word, choice of expression, relate more to the punctuation than to the pentameter.

But conversely exactly the same rules of pentameter and punctuation took Terry Hands towards a more rhetorical, declaimed set of solutions, most particularly in the brilliant partnership between him and Alan Howard. It seemed to me very important and very satisfying that the two complementary aspects of John's teaching were regularly on view, that the streams flowed apart and ran on side by side, and then came back together again.

One of the best things about life with the RSC and one of my most positive memories of it, was the extraordinary familial sense, and there are several reasons for it, not least the relationship between the theatre and the Flower family who of course were linked to it from its very foundation – and still are, as witness the traditional presence of Flower family members on its Board.

There was always a real sense in which the RSC was a nationally subsidized institution yet had an independence in its governing body and a Midlands rather than a national or metropolitan connection. This was a defining ingredient of its make-up.

Other things contributed – and still do – to the sense of family; the management team's relationship with each other, their relationship with the governing body, with the company, even with the town of Stratford itself, was like that in an extended family. There were not the usual divisions between work and home or between work and play.

At the RSC, the theatre is bound up with and connected to the whole of people's lives and I feel this particularly strongly now. When I get news of people leaving after thirty or forty years of service to the company I try to go to their leaving parties if I possibly can, or at the very least I write to them, and that is in no sense done as a chore; I feel these occasions to be family events and that I am making a trip back home. Of course I could be accused of sentimentality but I do firmly believe that there is a measurable sense of familial commitment in the RSC at Stratford. What you have is a huge nationally famous institution set in a relatively small community; many members of that community have devoted all their working lives to the theatre, which has given an identity to their lives and in turn the theatre takes on a sense of the identity of all those local people who have worked so selflessly for it. The fact that the theatre also acts as a considerable support to members of its family in times of trouble derives directly from this, and especially from the Flower family, because they felt about it, and about their own responsibility, in this way and their attitude has flowed through the organization. I don't know that this situation, with so many people in a local community devoting their entire working lifetimes to a theatre company, could ever be replicated anywhere else, or in the future.

I was always acutely aware that the company belonged to Stratford and that everything came back to that origin, for all that the RSC had a high-profile presence in London and a multi-million new home there at the Barbican, for all that it became an international company, touring in Europe, America, the Far East, Australia. The entire, diverse output of the RSC originated each year from the requirement, and indeed the passionate urge, to present a group of Shakespeare's plays. There could be no better conditions in which to do those plays than in the town of his birth, no better set of influences than those to be found there. Above all, in Stratford there is an absolutely unique audience. It is one that also poses a unique set of problems.

At any given time you could be performing to large numbers of people who had never seen the play before – indeed, to large numbers of people who had never been to a theatre before, but who might be sitting next to someone who had just written a book about the play. The challenge was to make things cohere for the whole audience, and never, ever say 'I'm terribly sorry but if you haven't studied this play closely and got a long way down the track in understanding it, and indeed, with Shakespeare in general, then this performance is not for you.' What we wanted to say instead was 'If you come inside this building you will be amazed to discover that Shakespeare is accessible to you and Shakespeare is thrilling, so much so that you will want to come back again ... and again.' But I was also adamant that we would never patronize our audience or talk down to them, never plead populism, and that what we were doing was equally valid to a group of Shakespeare scholars, or to the annual Summer School, or to a schools matinée.

By pleading populism, I mean doing Shakespeare in the way that the recent Baz Luhrmann film, *William Shakespeare's Romeo and Juliet* presents it; the director tries to find some externalized ways of making the narrative – and the narrative alone – exciting; visually the film is a triumph, but for all its title it is not the text of Shakespeare's *Romeo and Juliet* at all. We never placed ourselves in that situation; doing as much as possible of the text was the challenge.

To do Shakespeare any kind of justice you need to have an ensemble company because it is clear that you cannot do the work unless you spend considerable time on it, and unless you do several of the plays, taking into the next production what you have learned from the last.

To do Shakespeare in this way of course you need a larger group of people than would say an Ibsen or a Chekhov company and from that it follows that you have to offer them the possibility of training as well as working, training to get better at what they do, otherwise you are merely offering stasis and a wage packet.

Because there was a large ensemble company being trained and performing Shakespeare, that company wanted to do other things too (and there is the related question of having something to take up the slack of actors who are not working every night.)

All of which led, in fine, to The Other Place. It was becoming obvious that the influence of Fringe theatre was changing at the Edinburgh Festival, and similar work was also beginning to appear on the London scene, to the point where I organized two seasons of small scale work at a building called The Place in the Euston Road. At which point of course I asked myself why I was renting The Place in the Euston Road when in Stratford we had the building that we still called The Studio (erected as a temporary home for experiments to be conducted by Michel St. Denis) but which for the previous eight years had been used as a store.

The next step was a brief experiment done with Barry Kyle and Patrick Tucker, to see if we could make small-scale productions work in that space. We could! After that everything came together quite quickly: we got a licence, I appointed Buzz Goodbody to be the first Artistic Director to carry out an agreed policy – The Other Place was born. It was one of the most important things the RSC had done to date because it meant that genuine experiment with Shakespeare became a possibility. Immediately, Buzz Goodbody's own production of *Hamlet* – which was as fine as anything I have seen under that title – and a number of other small-scale Shakespeare productions directly fed the work (and the attitudes to the work) in the main house. It also led to a re-discovery of the neglected Shakespeare plays and to the policy of the production of new plays and then to a yearning to be able to re-discover and produce the whole of the Elizabethan and Jacobean repertoire.

What happened next culminated in something even more exciting. Those Elizabethan and Jacobean plays were on the whole not intimate works and so The Other Place was not a particularly good home for them. We needed a third auditorium. And the next dream was that of converting what was then the Conference Hall, our rehearsal room, back into the theatre it had originally been.

I nurtured that dream for a long time; how it eventually came to fulfillment is an extraordinary story. I managed to persuade the Governors to give me enough money to appoint an architect to develop the ideas contained in John Napier's sketch model to the designed-model stage (and it was very far-sighted of them to agree to it.) But in spite of exhaustive efforts here and in the United States, the fund-raising for the dream came to very little and the whole project was quite literally shelved – in a corner of the picture gallery, with a sad little notice in front of it saying 'Here is the theatre of our dreams – but we can't have it.'

There, one wet Saturday afternoon, an American gentleman came to shelter from the rain and look around. He saw the model, and asked who he should speak to about it and under-standably, everyone assumed that he was a passing journalist, an architectural student, a visiting scholar – absolutely nobody figured him for the billionaire and philanthropist Mr Frederick Koch! But, three days after that, I spread out the plans on the floor of his London flat and told him the full story of our dream and he said 'OK, we'll build that for you.'

The Swan Theatre cost our benefactor two million pounds. Perhaps if you allow simply for inflation it might cost double that to build it today – a new theatre. Yet I fear that in these days of building schemes funded by the National Lottery, there would be lots of people to tell you that The Swan should cost a great deal more

Yet having very little money means that you fight and fight for every possible way in which you can achieve the best but within your budget, you define and design simpler ways of doing things. It emphatically does not have to mean that you end up with second best and an inferior theatre. The Swan is something I am fantastically proud of; I think it is an amazingly beautiful space and a completely successful operation, and the fact that it has grown organically out of the old theatre in that cyclic way is particularly satisfying.

But if that is what I am most proud of, there has to be something I regret. It is unhelpful, I recognize, but what I regret profoundly is that the Barbican development ever crossed the RSC's path. In absolute contrast to the complete success of The Swan I think that the Barbican has not worked in the same way.

I inherited it. By the time I took over as Artistic Director in 1968, the Barbican was already a signed contract, a gift that could not be refused, and the way that things turned out could not have been predicted. But what the Barbican project meant was that for thirteen years I led a strange shadow existence in London which consisted of making decisions about, and supervising, a theatre that was only a plan on paper and a hole in the ground. Yet even at that stage my hands were more or less tied and I was told that everything was a fait accompli – I could not change anything except surfaces. I changed at least one of those for the better, after a tough battle, and the interior of the Barbican theatre is clad in the most beautiful dark wood as a result, and not the planned, near-white plastic-looking wood surface. I also managed to get rid of some nonsensically expensive stage technology that would have been as much of a white elephant as the great revolve in the Olivier theatre was, to begin with, at the National. I would very much have liked the Barbican theatre to have an orchestra pit but it was much too late for that. In theory it was also too late for us to have a second auditorium but eventually I did succeed in getting one, which threatened seriously to increase the cost of building because to change a plan is always more expensive than to originate one – it doubles the price. The auditorium called The Pit was only designated as a rehearsal room, so a space was there but in order for the ceiling height to be raised all the ductings had to be rerouted, major changes had to be made to provide a public entrance with lifts down to that level and so on. So, we achieved a second auditorium but at what cost? It was doomed to be vilified. It had taken years of fighting but I wonder whether the game was worth the candle. Would it have been better to accept the alternative option, of having our main auditorium at The Barbican and continuing to make the Donmar Warehouse in Covent Garden our second theatre, the London equivalent of The Other Place?

The Donmar Warehouse occupancy came about by another of those wonderful bits of serendipity with which I was blessed. The original and to me very exciting plan was to turn something which went by the delightful name of The Pooparts Warehouse into our small theatre, but local authority planning regulations finally scuppered that. When we had just three months to find a London home for The Other Place work David Brierley and I came out of Pooparts for the last time, defeated, and walked about miserably in Covent Garden, and as we did so we passed the old Donmar Rehearsal rooms that we had once used. We went in, and at once began to talk about how it might be turned into a theatre space. We called in the designer John Napier, who had drawn up the very first sketch plans showing how a theatre like The Swan might be made out of the Conference Hall, he almost instantaneously figured out an auditorium – and the Donmar Warehouse theatre was born.

The teeming activity of Covent Garden itself is another reason why I now think it would have been so much better for us to have kept our presence there in the Donmar. I had the task of convincing everyone that the Barbican would become a fine, lively late-night centre with shops and restaurants and other entertainments springing up all around it. That did not happen, despite the attempts which were made to make it happen. Everything militated against the Barbican as our theatre – the problem of getting there, the inhospitable nature of the approaches, the sheer difficulty of finding one's way around the building, all took their toll. There was a honeymoon period when things did go well for the RSC there, with excellent box office figures and some very exciting Shakespeare projects, the production of *Les Misérables*, Terry Hands's *Red Noses* – but after just three years the energy of all that began to flag and by the time that I left the RSC one could predict an uphill struggle to interest people in what was happening at the Barbican and attract a good audience down there.

If I regret the Barbican, which I do, and if I am proud of The Swan, which I am, there is a third thing, something of which I am equally proud and which I never regretted for a moment – the RSC's annual extended visit or residency to Newcastle, which became our northern home.

Once I had had the idea, it became an obsession, but one in which I was wholeheartedly supported by the then financial controller, Bill Wilkinson and above all again by David Brierley, the best theatre administrator in the country until his recent retirement and a man who, for all his absolute sense of responsibility and innate caution, did not have the word 'no' in his vocabulary.

Newcastle came about because I felt strongly that we were wasting our time and spending precious energies and huge resources touring the country, stopping for a week here and a week there, putting down no roots, laying claim to nobody's loyalty. If a production had had a great deal of national publicity or if we had a film or television star on board, we could sometimes attract a respectable audience, but what was it all supposed to mean to the places we were visiting?

Then I asked what a company like the Berliner Ensemble would do in the circumstances. The answer was that they would choose another city carefully and then move their whole national operation there for a period. That was what I felt we should do.

We already had our Headquarters in the Midlands and a London base, so it was clear that we must find somewhere to display our work in the North. The city had to be at the centre of a large catchment area, preferably to be at the heart of a conurbation with many centres of population within striking distance. It could not be Manchester, which already had the Royal Exchange Theatre – and we were not going to threaten anybody else's enterprises – and the same applied to Liverpool, with The Playhouse and the Everyman.

Newcastle was the obvious choice. It fitted the bill in every way geographically and it had a magnificent theatre but not much by way of a permanent company presence. Our commitment to Newcastle, when we made it, was that we would take them everything, our main house repertoire, our Other Place Repertoire, late night shows, lunchtime shows, new training work, education work, going out to schools and colleges and bringing them in to us, and that we would continue to do so year after year. Newcastle was to become our permanent Northern home.

From my personal point of view, Newcastle was wonderful – I loved everything about it, the theatre, the place, the people, the friends we made there, even the bitter north east wind, familiar to me anyhow, as I was born an east coaster, albeit a little further down in Suffolk!

One of the reasons why Newcastle always worked out so well is that by the time the long Stratford season was over and we were about to go up there the company had welded firmly together as a unit. That has something to do first of all with the smallness of Stratford, the fact that you can walk to anybody else's house and walk from anybody's house down to the theatre, that you live in a village-like community and share your lives there. (So many people who once worked with the Company have gone on to buy properties there or return to live permanently in the area, because Stratford represents a mixture of living and working that is on exactly the right scale; it is unforced. It is a very happy time.)

During the course of the season people have worked together in different ratios and relationships in a large space, a medium space and a small space, each of which makes different demands upon them, in each of which they have to place a different sort of reliance upon one another. Your interdependency is huge in the vast main theatre when you are projecting out to 1600 people and it is equally important but quite different in The Other Place, when what happens behind your eyelid is communicating itself to every single person in that tiny auditorium. Any lack of commitment from your colleague in either situation will strand you and make you feel both idiotic and very exposed.

With all this as a background the company arrived in Newcastle as an inseparable body and the strength of that was tremendous and made a powerful impact upon the place from day one.

I have looked at my time with the RSC, and that time is past, I have talked about what seem to me to have been the highlights, of success and failure, of the things I am most proud of and the thing that I regret. I am not directly involved in the future of the company but I think a lot about it, and I think that I know absolutely what it must continue to stand for and why it is so very important as we approach the next century. We live in a very fast-changing world. I referred earlier to the most recent mega-success with Shakespeare on film, *William Shakespeare's Romeo and Juliet*; it has been far more successful than any other concurrent attempts at a Shakespeare film. But all of the others attempted in their very different ways to present the text of the play on film; the most popular one, the most successful in commercial terms, only used the text as a sort of jumping-off point. The message it gave out was that 'this is an old work and we are modernizing it to try and attract and hold your attention.' Beyond that there is no interest in any way whatsoever in illuminating the text, in inquiring what that text might be able to tell us now, or in exploring it in terms of its ambiguity, say, or its wit. That is evidence, and sad evidence to me, of a world where culturally as well as in every other way, people want rapid results and fast impressions, sound-bites, quick-changing images, and do not on the whole want the bother of concentrating hard for long periods.

I am worried that this will mean that a Shakespeare theatre will have a very real struggle to inspire and excite the young to have the kind of interest we have taken for granted over generations, without doing the craven things I have just described.

Therefore it seems to me that Stratford at this moment is symbolically more important than at any other point in its history, that Stratford has got to be declared the Shakespeare centre of the world, that so far as the Royal Shakespeare Company is concerned nothing else matters. Whatever systems are invented to get the artists to work there, whatever has to be done to keep the insatiable theatrical inquiry into Shakespeare and the presentation of Shakespeare of the highest integrity, must be done.

Because Stratford has the responsibility of taking all these fundamental assumptions of ours into the next century.

* The text is an edited version of a taped interview with Trevor Nunn

'Come sing and you that will not,
hold your tongues.'

GUY WOOLFENDEN

The RSC was casting *The Tempest*. A young Scottish actor was offered the part of Ferdinand, but no suitable candidate for Ariel had emerged. The director, Clifford Williams, heard a rumour that the young Scot had a fine singing voice and suggested that he might consider swapping roles, subject to me, as the composer, auditioning him. On arriving at the company's London rehearsal rooms – a converted banana warehouse in Floral Street, Covent Garden – I was introduced to Ian Charleson. 'Have you brought any music with you, and would you like me to accompany you?' I enquired. 'No, thanks all the same', he replied courteously, and, passing the piano, Ian briefly touched a note, walked purposefully into the centre of the space and started to sing 'My love is like a red, red rose' very affectingly. 'He'll never get that high note near the start of the second phrase,' I remember thinking, but he floated it with consummate skill and intuitive musicianship. Clifford Williams offered Ian the part there and then, and another young lion, Alan Rickman joined the cast as Ferdinand.

A few months ago I heard this audition story recounted on the BBC series Private Passions by Genista McIntosh, then RSC casting director, who was listening just outside the rehearsal room door, and was much moved by the experience. After a distinguished career with the RSC and RNT, Jenny was until recently Chief Executive of the Royal Opera House, which will brought her into contact with all those superb performers whose singing voices are their passports to fame and fortune, but in the straight theatre different rules apply.

Here the singing voice has to take second place to the speaking voice. A great 'tone deaf' actor is more highly prized than a second-stringer with a mellifluous baritone. Very occasionally, as in the case of Ian Charleson, the singing and the speaking voices are discovered to be of equal quality and *Hamlet* and Sky Masterson (in *Guys and Dolls*) are both considered sensible casting possibilities, not to mention the leading role in an Oscar-winning movie, *Chariots of Fire*. All these parts followed Ian's début as Ariel at the RST in 1978.

I am very clear in my own mind how to set about casting most of the singing roles in the Shakespeare canon. To take two prime examples: Amiens in *As You Like It* and Ophelia in *Hamlet*. Amiens is a forest lord who, with his songs, guides us through the emotional and climatic seasons of the play. He should be a specialist singer, able to move us with the stark images of 'Blow, blow, thou winter wind' or make us envy the delights of an escapist life 'Under the Greenwood Tree'. The part of Ophelia, on the other hand, simply has to be given to the most talented young actress in the company, who can cope with the vast emotional range of the part, and sing with conviction, but not necessarily in a voice that would charm the birds out of the trees. As her wits desert her, Ophelia is given to chanting 'snatches of old lauds' with almost unbearably poignant buried references to her recently slaughtered father, and shockingly, for a young virgin, she coins filthy double meanings to the seemingly innocent rhymes which signal her other loss: the love of Hamlet. The acting element required in the successful performance of those songs far outweighs the need of an intrinsically beautiful singing voice. Nor, in my opinion, does it help when composers draw attention to themselves by writing impossibly difficult 'mad songs'. It is so much more effective when Ophelia distorts either the familiar traditional tunes, or new settings composed in an unpretentiously simple idiom.

I have been very privileged to have worked with several memorable Ophelias: Glenda Jackson, followed by Janet Suzman and Estelle Kohler for Peter Hall's production with David Warner as Hamlet in 1965, Helen Mirren for Trevor Nunn in 1970, starring Alan Howard, and more recently Joanne Pearce in Adrian Noble's production in 1992 (with Kenneth Branagh warming up for his amazing four-hour film version). I even became briefly involved in the Franco Zeffirelli/Mel Gibson film helping Helena Bonham Carter with her songs.

Some directors make a convincing case for one or two of the songs to be accompanied. Peter Hall encouraged me to teach his Ophelias to play simple accompaniments on the lute – in fact, a lute guitar, that is strung like a guitar but has a lute belly – which, because of its evocative shape, was used at one point in the production as a potent symbol of the child she would never bear. In Trevor Nunn's production Christopher Gable as Laertes gave brotherly musical support to Helen Mirren.

Adrian Noble went even further, and persuaded me to write piano accompaniments for some of the songs. The production style was updated to the turn of the century, and Ophelia's bed-room furniture included a dear little painted upright. 'How should I your true love know' became a major leitmotif, and indeed Adrian's vision for the end of that production featured the piano alone on stage in a ghostly spotlight seemingly play-ing by itself. We had, in the end, to settle for a recording as neither the complicated technology of a pianola mechanism with a specially cut paper roll, nor the latest Japanese 'syn-clavier' electronics, could be fitted into the tiny instrument.

It has long been an RSC tradition, when the dramatic situa-tion demands it, that actors learn to play instruments that are part of their character assumption. In *Julius Caesar* it is unthink-able to me that Lucius, Brutus's slave, should mime to an off-stage lyre, or, even worse, a tape recording, for the 'sleepy tune' he plays to comfort his master the night before the battle of Philippi. Generations of actors have learnt to play a succes-sion of doctored auto-harps (a sort of zither), but eventually Michael Tubbs, Director of Music at the RST, made a beautiful Roman lyre, which has graced the stage in many productions, most recently played by Daniel Goode for Peter Hall in 1995.

Michael also designed an authentic-looking Egyptian Harp which Sidney Livingstone as Mardian the eunuch played so sensitively in Trevor Nunn's 1972 production of *Antony and Cleopatra* in response to the summons:

> Give me some music: music, moody food
> Of us that trade in love.

One of the finest actor-singer-instrumentalists to tread the boards at Stratford during the last thrity years was Emrys James. A definitive Feste in John Barton's 1969 production of *Twelfth Night* accompanying himself on the lute-guitar with conviction;

a sinister and seductive Iago to Brewster Mason's Othello, with a deftly wielded concertina for the 'King Stephen' song; and who will forget his deeply troubled Parson Hugh Evans singing:

> To shallow rivers, to whose falls
> Melodious birds sing madrigals

while waiting for the fiery Doctor Caius to turn up for the duel that's not to be, on the lonely field near Frogmore, in Terry Hands's celebrated production of *The Merry Wives of Windsor*.

Other favourites include, of course, Ben Kingsley, who as Ariel even composed his own songs, and music-lovers Norman Rodway and Joe Melia, whose knowledge of classical music off stage, and ability to perform popular music on stage, is awe-inspiring. Derek Smith also made his mark, most memorably in Trevor Nunn's 1970 production of *The Winter's Tale*, as an endearing, hippy Autolycus.

Some great actors confess that they have no ear for music and don't even wish to sing, be cast in a singing role, or forced into a situation where singing is a prerequisite of accepting the part. Two that spring to mind – John Carlisle and Donald Sinden – have something else in common: speaking voices of great range, variety, beauty, colour and nuance. Donald can pipe in a strange upper register, and 'roar you as gently as any sucking dove', or plumb the Chaliapin depths in an amazing downward swoop. John can command an almost Dietrich Fischer-Dieskau-like legato of great beauty, but both are excused singing duties, even when the whole company is on stage giving voice!

That much-loved Stratford-upon-Avon personality, Denne Gilkes, singing coach and landlady to the stars – Vanessa

Redgrave and Paul Scofield, for example – was reputed to be able to teach anybody or anything to sing – except perhaps a lamp-post. After Donald Sinden's first lesson, Denne phoned Paddy Donnell (then the RST general manager) to inform him that she had found her lamp-post!

Donald's somewhat sketchy appreciation of rhythm and melody did, however, on one occasion, work to his advantage. Cast as Henry VIII, Trevor Nunn plotted him to be alone on stage in the 'Holbein' pose, looking perplexed in the dumb show which began that production. As Donald had considerable difficulty remembering which beat of the bar was his cue to move off stage, before the lights changed and the scenery moved, his perplexed look carried tremendous conviction and authority, which several critics picked up in their extremely appreciative notices!

Shakespeare's practical approach in play after play to the potential problems of actors whose voices may not be quite up to standard, or might be hoarse with coughs and colds from inhaling those Bankside fogs, has always greatly impressed me. Consider this exchange between Amiens and Jaques:

AMIENS: My voice is ragged; I know I cannot please you.
JAQUES: I do not desire you to please me, I do desire you to sing.

That should get Amiens off the hook if he's having an off-night, but if he sings the second stanza of the song triumphantly well, Amiens' disclaimer comes across merely as the traditional false modesty of the practised performer, and Jaques' remark is absolutely in character for that world-weary misanthrope.

Similar exchanges of this nature abound: Don Pedro in *Much Ado About Nothing* tries to compliment the musician Balthazar in his performance of 'Sigh no more ladies', the latter having already informed us that there's not a note of his that's worth the noting.

DON PEDRO: By my troth, a good song.
BALTHAZAR: And an ill singer, my lord.
CLAUDIO: Ha, no, no, faith; thou singest well enough for a shift.

Benedick, who is hidden during the song, further covers the possibility of Balthazar having an off-night with some humour but little finesse: 'An he had been a dog that should have howled thus, they would have hanged him; and I pray God his bad voice bode no mischief.'

Unbroken boys' voices can be vulnerable to hormones, the weather, sore throats, or sheer incompetence, and the Bard has answers to all these problems too. At the end of the pages' song 'It was a lover and his lass' from *As You Like It* Touchstone says 'God buy you, and God mend your voices!' – another practical get-out clause if things go awry!

As well as covering up for the possible shortcomings of his actor/singers, Shakespeare also had an odd habit of entrusting some of his most charming lyrics to the hastily assembled musical ensembles of despised and unworthy suitors. In *Cymbeline*, the boorish Cloten assembles the necessary forces to perform the sublime dawn chorus 'Hark, hark! the lark at heaven's gate sings' to serenade the matchless Imogen, which, of course, she disdainfully ignores.

The unsuitable Thurio, outmanoeuvred by the unscrupulous Proteus, is responsible for the equally exquisite 'Who is Silvia?' in *The Two Gentlemen of Verona*, which likewise fails to impress the heroine. In David Thacker's 1991 production of the play, I was obliged to compose 'Who is Silvia?' in the style of George Gershwin, as the production was set in the early 1930s, with an on-stage band, and a singer – the excellent Hilary Cromie – perched on a bar stool, crooning all those unforgettable 'evergreen' American hit songs of the period.

American musicals from *Show Boat* to Sondheim were once the envy of the rest of the world but, since the Andrew Lloyd Webber cycle, and the success of the Claude Michel Schonberg/Alain Boubil trilogy, the torch seems to have crossed to this side of the Atlantic. No small thanks to English directors who have worked with great distinction at the RSC. Trevor Nunn's contribution to *Cats*, *Starlight Express*, *Aspects of Love* and *Sunset Boulevard* is an inestimable creative achievement, as was his co-production for the RSC with John Caird of *Les Misérables*. Nick Hytner directed *Miss Saigon* with great flair, and Sam Mendes revived Lionel Bart's *Oliver* and Stephen Sondheim's *Company* to considerable critical acclaim. Almost all these productions featured leading RSC actors with singing voices that not only totally satisfied the demands of their various roles, but also stood up to the intense pressure of long runs in the West End.

Roger Allam was the original Jean Valjean and Alun Armstrong the Host in *Les Misérables* at the Barbican. Roger went on to appear in *City of Angels*, and Alun also made his mark in *The Baker's Wife* and as the eponymous anti-hero in *Sweeney Todd*. Jonathan Pryce gave his surveyor in *Miss Saigon*, Fagin in *Oliver* and more recently General Peron in the film of *Evita*, and Brian Blessed appeared as Old Deuteronomy in *Cats*. Incidentally, but for a damaged Achilles tendon which obliged her to retire from the role of Grizabella, Dame Judi Dench would have been entrusted with singing 'Memory' – Trevor Nunn's inspired response to Andrew Lloyd Webber's hit number.

How has this flowering of vocal talent occurred? Why don't the RSC do more musicals? Without the generous profit participation that Trevor helped to secure for the RSC from his production of *Les Misérables*, the company would certainly not have been able to mount the impressive number of productions that it has achieved over the last decade. At one point over twenty revivals of the piece were paying their Dane-geld to us.

Yes, we have had successful and enjoyable productions of *Poppy* from Terry Hands, *Kiss me Kate* from Adrian Noble and a most interesting co-production with Opera North of *Show Boat*, brilliantly directed by Ian Judge, but neither of these last two were really able to make great use of regular RSC actors, if you exclude brilliant cameos from Trevor Peacock as Cap'n Andy in *Show Boat* and John Bardon as one of the 'Brush Up Your Shakespeare' gangsters in *Kiss me Kate*. Ian Judge also presented two revivals of *The Wizard of Oz* with strong all-dancing, all-singing casts, and John Caird's *The Beggar's Opera*, arranged by Ilona Sekacz, was extremely strong on its musical casting (David Burt a potent Macheath) in the Swan Theatre in 1992.

Received opinion from Shaftesbury Avenue and Broadway suggests that perhaps the days of the blockbuster musical are numbered, and we should let Saigons be Saigons, but I'm not so sure. Meanwhile, I shall continue to try to persuade the RSC to produce *Dogs*, a Tarantino-inspired version of *101 Dalmatians*, which I have in my bottom drawer. What do you mean, have I lost my marbles? We had a go at *Carrie*, didn't we?

Whilst actors seem able to transform themselves into musical comedy stars with increasing frequency, the reverse journey, from famous singer into straight actor, is a less common occurrence. But in 1989, during a blisteringly hot summer,

Willard White, that noble Wagnerian bass-baritone, fresh from his triumph in *Porgy and Bess* at Glyndebourne, turned up on his mountain bike to rehearse Trevor Nunn's *Othello* in the last major production at The Other Place, before it was rebuilt.

Incidentally, isn't it odd that a great composer like Verdi hears Iago as a bass and Otello as a tenor, albeit one with a dark voice like Placido Domingo. Trevor Nunn, of course, cast it the other way round: *Othello*, the bass, tortured by the suspected treachery of Desdemona and using all those low pitched resonances, with Iago, one of McKellen's greatest performances, needling away in a higher register. I have always been very sensitive to this little discussed area of RSC casting, and sometimes find that actors with matching timbres and a similar vocal range who are obliged to play long scenes together, are tiring to listen to and unconvincing for purely musical reasons. Experienced BBC Radio Drama directors seldom make this mistake!

I love the company of actors. I love to hear them tell their wonderfully exaggerated theatrical anecdotes with all the skills of the practised raconteur. I can even enjoy regular doses of their small talk, but above all, I admire their sheer nerve and bravery. To go on stage night after night requires great courage. Sir Laurence Olivier suffered agonies of stage fright and crossing the last few feet from the darkness of the wings to the blaze of the stage could be a great torture to him. The skills actors strive to acquire to fulfil the demands of a particular role involve specific forms of bravery. For example: the physical skill and considerable discipline needed to master armed and unarmed combat with total conviction, and scrupulous regard to the safety of fellow actors. A different sort of courage and discipline is required to take one's clothes off without being embarrassed or causing embarrassment. A certain degree of chutzpah is involved in wearing clothes that are unflattering, unsightly and uncomfortable, and making them look convincing on stage. It takes fortitude to appear when you are ill and your understudy is also poorly, unprotected by those apologies that are all too common in the opera house. Private grief, bereavement, lost love, even divorce, have to be overcome in the service of the performance and its ever demanding public. As a musician, though I am deeply sensitive to all these manifestations of theatrical bravery, the sheer guts involved when actors have to sing on stage, often after whole acts of using their speaking voices with maximum projection, is still near the top of my list. But when the nerves settle, and the singing becomes second nature, a rare joy can be generated on the stage and can flood over the footlights, in a way that is special to straight theatre.

For me this happened triumphantly in Trevor Nunn's 1976 production of *The Comedy of Errors*, which was presented as a musical, and cast entirely from the talented company who were in residence in Stratford that season. Trevor wrote the witty lyrics, based on, and often quoting, Shakespeare's lines. John Napier devised an ingenious modern set, which served every twist of the plot expertly. Gillian Lynne was responsible for the imaginative musical staging, which involved everyone in the company undertaking serious training and using muscle groups they weren't aware they possessed. I composed the score as fast as I was able, sometimes limping behind Trevor, who had a short head start with the lyrics.

A simple rule was established as to who got to sing a number and who was excused. Anyone who professed, without false modesty, to not having a reasonable voice or any ambition to sing a solo, was excused. Luckily the cast was full of actors with vocal promise and expertise, for example: Judi Dench (Adriana), Francesca Annis (Luciana), Michael Williams (Dromio of Syracuse), Roger Rees (Antipholus of Syracuse) and Robin Ellis (Dr. Pinch).

Nickolas Grace (Dromio of Ephesus), who has a fine voice, somehow got left out, and took to hanging round the piano after rehearsals and leaving pointed notes in pigeon holes suggesting places where a show-stopping number for his character could fit in. Eventually, he succeeded in persuading Trevor to write a lyric about how his master was given, on the slightest pretext, to slapping and kicking him for any misdemeanour. The resulting song: 'Beats Me' did indeed stop the show on many occasions and Nick Grace went on to perform with distinction in other musicals including Bernstein's *Candide*.

But what I, and everyone who saw the show, will never forget, was the power of the big ensemble numbers in which everyone had to sing. The opening chorus 'Beg thou or borrow' which revealed both concern and indifference for Aegeon (Griffith Jones), in his bid to ransom himself before nightfall:

> Try all the friends that thou hast in Ephesus,
> You'll find there's nobody quite so deaf as us!

The brilliantly choreographed snip-snap movement and razor sharp reactions to Robin Ellis's amazing rendition of Dr. Pinch's exorcism number 'Satan come forth', were a wonder to behold. But the unstoppable joy of the finale, 'Hand in Hand', when all the ravelled ends of that wondrously ingenious plot are finally knitted together, brought the show to an ecstatic conclusion, and on a good night was one of the happiest RSC experiences of my long time with the company.

The Comedy of Errors won an Ivor Novello Award and a Society of West End Theatre Award as the Best British Musical of the year, was televised and published as a video and is still performed world wide. However, no company, not even my beloved RSC, have come up with such an effective first night publicity stunt as the Nye Theatre in Oslo a few years ago. They offered free tickets to any pairs of twins who applied for them, provided each couple agreed to turn up in matching or similar costumes. The foyer before the show was full of members of the audience rubbing their eyes, checking their spectacles and vowing never to touch another drop of alcohol, but as soon as the krone dropped, the theatregoers of Oslo (previously unfamiliar with Shakespeare's profligate deployment – pace Plautus – of two sets of twins) were absolutely delighted by the play and their theatre's opening night stunt.

In over thirty years with the RSC I have been most heartened by the overall improvement of the singing skills of our actors. Conversely, in the opera house, the acting has greatly improved from the 'stand and deliver' style of yesteryear. The efforts of our drama and music colleges, coupled with the demands of the profession, and its directors, plus the explosion of the blockbuster musical, have all contributed to this advance. Long may it continue.

INTERLUDE

A Round of Drinks with John Barton

DONALD SINDEN

I think I have learned more from John Barton as a director and as a friend than from any other person. I am not academic and I inordinately admire John, who is. I pick his brains unashamedly. I have always had a love for the English language and it thrilled me to find in John someone with a vastly superior knowledge who could guide my inexperienced steps. Just as a small insight into the way his mind works, I am told that in 1961 he was asked, in an emergency to devise an anthology to be performed at the RSC's new London home, The Aldwych Theatre. Having decided that the theme should be the Kings and Queens of England as seen through their own and contemporary writings, he was able from memory to direct an assistant to the exact works in which all the myriad references were to be found. The result was enormously successful. *The Hollow Crown* is still being performed all over the world.

Of course there are times when I disagree with him or question his theories; the instance, the yardstick that he applies to all actors is Hamlet's advice to the players:

Speak the speech, I pray you, as I pronounced it to you, trippingly on the tongue; but if you mouth it as many of your fellows do, I had as lief the town crier spoke my lines.

So far so good, but John also claims to know how English was spoken at the time of Shakespeare and one of his party pieces is to recite Henry the Fifth's 'Once more unto the breach dear friends, once more ...' in the way it is believed to have been spoken in Elizabethan England. The sound is very like a strong Somerset accent. The word 'more' is pronounced 'mawerr' and can only be achieved by mouthing it. If Hamlet's advice is spoken in the same Zummerzet burr it makes complete nonsense of 'trippingly on the tongue.'

Again, John can be quite devious. In *Henry VI Part* 2, Jack Cade interrogates a Clerk from Clapham:

What is thy name?
Emmanuel.
They use it to write on the top of letters ... away with him I say: hang him with his pen and ink-horn about his neck.

I was mystified by this exchange; I failed to understand it and plucked up courage to ask John, 'What does it mean?'
'What?'
'Emmanuel – they use to write it on the top of letters.'
'It's quite clear isn't it?'
'Not to me.'
'You mean he is not saying it correctly?'
'No – I don't understand it.'
'What? "Emmanuel – they use to write it on the top of letters?"'
'Yes.'

'Surely it means what it says.'

'Yes, but you know I'm stupid. Why does he say that they used to write Emmanuel on the top of letters?'

Someone less brave than I would have given in at John's expression, but I faced him out. His look softened and he said, 'As a matter of fact, I don't know.'

Rehearsal rooms are minefields to John and where there are no mines there are snares and traps. Everyone else is aware of the hazards but not he. It is customary for a long trestle table to be set up facing the acting area; behind it, bang in the centre, sits the director, flanked by various members of the stage management and technical staff. John is forever jumping up to discuss something with an actor or to re-arrange the positions – he seems to have 110 per cent concentration and becomes oblivious to the presence of those on either side, with the result that he regularly collides with chairs or people. Some stage-managers have tried to overcome the problem by having two tables – one for John and one for them. This fact seems to have eluded John who then tries to avoid imaginary chairs and has even been known to go over or under the table in his haste.

He always wears a thick chunky cardigan and absent-mindedly produces unlikely things from the pockets. When he was trying to give up smoking he produced a wrapped razor-blade from a pocket and proceeded to munch it.

When rehearsals move onto the stage, life becomes even more precarious. A short flight of wooden steps is placed to allow access to the stage from the lower auditorium. It is also a habit of some people to place coffee cups along the edge of the stage so, knowing that John is on the rampage, the stage-manager makes sure that none is in his line of access, but he will choose that time to avoid the steps and jump up onto the stage.

The clever stage-manager remembers to have a mopping-up cloth to hand. On leaving the stage John merely hurls himself at the auditorium, sometimes missing the steps entirely. He was once giving notes at the end of a rehearsal and stepping backwards, disappeared down the orchestra pit ... All the actors rushed forward to render first-aid but John climbed out obliviously, clutching his papers and continued to give his notes. It is the actors who suffer nervous breakdowns.

And this was the man, remember, staying in our house.

One morning he said plaintively, 'Diana, have you seen any of my shirts? I can't find any.'

Diana had expected him to look after his own laundry but that morning, after he had left the house, she went to his room, and, under the bed, behind the chest of drawers. on top of the wardrobe, she found twenty-three dirty shirts. These she took to the fastest laundry in Stratford. Three weeks later John said plaintively, 'Diana, have you seen any of my shirts? I can't find any.' Again, under the bed, behind the chest of drawers, on top of the wardrobe, Diana found twenty-three shirts. But this time she found inside each neck-band a laundry ticket attached with two safety-pins. He had worn the shirts with no sign of discomfort.

A colleague and fellow-director of John's – David Jones – told me that for a time he had shared the Barton flat in London. Entering the kitchen he found that a kettle had not only boiled dry on the gas-stove but a hole had burned through the bottom of it. A worried David decided he had the answer to John's problem and bought him an electric kettle which turned itself off after boiling. When John came home and saw it, he was despondent; 'Oh dear – I wish you hadn't done that – what am I to do with these?' He opened a cupboard and there were fourteen new ordinary kettles, all ready for the next burned-out bottom.

I have left the most astonishing Bartonism till last. People don't believe it, but I assure you it is true.

During rehearsals and during performances, John is always giving notes. Of course it is wonderful to have someone who cares as much as he, but no actor can escape – he will hunt you down. He has been known to beard a nervous actor in his dressing room twenty minutes before the play is due to start – on a first night – and give his notes on quite a different play.

He soon discovered that several of the company popped across to the Dirty Duck during their one-hour-exactly lunch break from rehearsals – what a perfect place to ensnare his prey. He took to wandering around the bar only taking his eyes from his notebook long enough to spy his next victim. Hoping to distract him, actors would invite him to have a drink – but to no avail. He accepted and continued his tracking, glass in hand.

Someone in the management pointed out to him that he had received a number of drinks, but was getting a bad reputation because he never bought any in return. John was horrified and that very lunch-time he raced across to the Duck, flung open the door and announced to a bar full of astonished strangers, 'Drinks are on me.' He made a mental note of each requirement and reeled off the list to the bar-maid. 'Three whiskeys – two with soda, one with water; four gin and tonics; four vodkas – two with tomato juice, two with bitter lemon; one Guinness; five halves of bitter; two pints; four halves of cider; one brandy and ginger ale; and two bitter lemons.' The order was placed on a circular tray and John was asked for 'Four pounds, eighteen and ninepence.' He then picked up the tray and turned;

forgetting that he had put his foot over the brass rail ...
Twenty-four glasses and their contents crashed to the floor.

John immediately turned back to the barmaid and said, ' Oh
dear. Same again please; three whiskeys, two with soda, one
with water; four gin and tonics; four vodkas – two with tomato juice, two with bitter lemon; one Guinness; five halves of
bitter; two pints; two halves of cider; one brandy and ginger ale;
and two bitter lemons.' Meanwhile the assembly had picked up
the broken glass. The barmaid started to tot up.

'That will be, er ...'

'Four pounds, eighteen and ninepence,' interjected John. He
picked up the tray and – yes – he had again forgotten his foot
in the rail. Down went another twenty-four glasses and their
contents.

'Oh dear – I'm so sorry – same again please; three whiskeys
– two with soda, one with water ...'

By now the bar was awash and in a state of turmoil. 'That
should be four pounds, eighteen and ninepence,' said John, but
before he could lift the tray he was surrounded by a group of
helping hands. He was most indignant. 'I can manage perfectly
well, thank you.' He extricated his foot and carried the tray in a
most dignified manner to a low, round table in the middle of
the room and placed it carefully. 'There – you see?!' He sat
down at the settle, crossed his legs triumphantly – and kicked
over the tray-laden table.

FIFTY YEARS

FROM THE RECORDS, FOR THE RECORD

The Plays

The following is a list of all Shakespeare's plays in order of the number of times they have been produced in the Stratford theatres (excluding any Theatre in Education productions) during the past fifty years.

The Theatres

Fifty years ago there was one theatre. Now there are three, and the second, The Swan grew literally out of the first.

What is now known as The Main House was conceived as The Shakespeare Memorial Theatre in 1875. As secretary to the local committee Charles Flower wrote:

This is an opportune time for renewing the project which was proposed in 1864 for erecting a suitable monument to Shakespeare in his native town, and that monument should take the form of a Memorial Theatre, a building which, inside and out, should be completely adapted for its object, and as architecturally ornamental as possible.

The original architects, Unsworth and Dodgson, were selected from 31 designs in open competition and their first was submitted under the title from *Romeo and Juliet* 'What here shall miss our toil shall strive to mend.' That was adapted and resubmitted for the competition final as (from *Henry IV Part 2*) 'But to the purpose and so to the venture.'

Their prize was 25 guineas for a building to evoke a mixture of Gothic and Tudor styles and the foundation stone was laid on Shakespeare's birthday, 23 April 1877.

There were two principal parts to the building. First the auditorium, the stage and the dressing rooms, and the second, the gallery (as it still exists in 1997) and the library. The final cost on completion (in 1881) came to £20,000, the original seating capacity was 658 and the building was opened, also on the Birthday, 23 April 1879, with a performance of *Much Ado About Nothing*.

On 6 March 1926 the building was gutted by fire.

After the building of the new Shakespeare Memorial Theatre, a conversion of the shell of the old was used as a fine conference hall and rehearsal space until the final conversion into a second auditorium, The Swan, took place (the story of which is told by Trevor Nunn earlier in this book)

The Swan finally opened with a production of *The Two Noble Kinsmen* on May 8 1986. It is a new theatre yet it has grown organically out of the old and the symbol of the fact is the great wisteria planted in Charles Flower's day which has been carefully preserved and still flourishes on the old wall.

Its 10th anniversary was celebrated in May 1996 with fireworks.

The third RSC auditorium is a new building now but it too evolved from the old one on the same site. The Other Place had humble origins as a corrugated iron shed in the paddock in Southern Lane which runs up from Waterside. It was to be a studio theatre and the original tentative sketches for it were done as far back as 1964, the year of the Shakespeare Quatercentenary, but that year also marked the beginning of discussions on the London Barbican project and plans for a studio space in Stratford went onto the back burner.

Thereafter the history of The Other Place is one of continuing controversy and when Buzz Goodbody was appointed
the first Artistic Director in 1973 and submitted her vision of
the alternative theatre, there was considerable opposition to
the project, which meant that TOP had to be self-funded and
managed within extremely tight restrictions – none of the plays
in the opening season, which included *The Tempest* and *Uncle
Vanya*, was allowed a budget of more than 200.

It opened first in 1974 with an adaptation of *King Lear* devised for schools by Buzz Goodbody, and seated, in the basic
corrugated hut, 140 people in some discomfort. Conditions
were no better for the actors. There was no flying space and no
trap at this time and actors making entrances at the far end of
the hall had to brave all the elements.

The turning point for TOP came in 1985, after the huge success of productions of *The Dillen*, which included local people
in the cast and made a perambulation about the town, stopping
to act scenes at various points along Avonbank and in Old
Town. It attracted huge support and as a result The Friends of
The Other Place was founded to raise money for improve-
ments and amenities. (Until then the same washroom had been
used by both actors and audience and every year fire, health
and safety officials threatened the theatre with closure.)

There was more local controversy in 1985 when the RSC
sold land around the Southern Lane paddock – part of the
inheritance from Charles Flower and long-time home of the
Stratford Tennis Club – and made plans to use the funds for a
more permanent building.

Trevor Nunn's production of *Othello* was the final one in the
old corrugated hut Other Place in the summer of 1988.

Original design ideas for the new theatre had been radical,

possibly in hexagonal or octagonal shape, but it was finally decided to preserve the style of the old building and blend it with the new. Originally it seated 240 people but in 1996 new seating arrangements were made and the capacity is now 170.

A Diary

1948   Artistic Director – Sir Barry Jackson
1949   Anthony Quayle appointed as Artistic Director
1952   Glen Byam Shaw appointed as Artistic Director
         with Quayle
1953–54 Anthony Quayle leads a tour to Australia and New
         Zealand with Barbara Jefford
1953–54 Barbara Jefford appointed an assistant Artistic
         Director
1958   Peter Hall appointed assistant director to Glen
         Byam Shaw.
         An important tour of *Romeo and Juliet*, *Twelfth Night*
         and *Hamlet* to Moscow and Leningrad, sponsored
         by The British Council
1959–60 The 100th season. Peter Hall appointed Artistic
         Director. He declares his intention of forming a
         more permanent company of actors with a dis-
         cernible policy of verse speaking and acting.
1960   The RSC'S London home, at The Aldwych

	Theatre, inaugurated, with a performance of Webster's *The Duchess of Malfi* starring Peggy Ashcroft.
1961–62	Triumvirate of Artistic Directors. Peter Brook, Peter Hall and Michel Saint-Denis
1964	June 18th. Royal Command performance of *The Comedy of Errors* in the Waterloo Chamber, Windsor Castle.

November. A recital given by company members Dorothy Tutin, Tony Church and Derek Godfrey in the Vatican. This is the first time the Pope has ever been to a theatrical performance.

1964–65	*The Wars of the Roses* recorded. *The Hollow Crown* shown on American television.
1966–67	Start of TheatreGoRound at the studio theatre to promote live theatre in schools, colleges and community centres.
1967–68	The last of the Peter Hall years as Artistic Director
1968	Trevor Nunn Artistic Director. Peter Hall becomes Managing Director
1968–77	Trevor Nunn assisted by Peter Hall, Peter Brook and Peggy Ashcroft
1973–86	Peter Hall is Consultant Director
1978–86	Artistic Directors Trevor Nunn and Terry Hands, assisted by John Barton, Peggy Ashcroft and Peter Brook
1978	Opening of The Warehouse in London (190 seats)
1986	Opening of The Swan
1986–91	Terry Hands Artistic Director and Chief Executive, advised by Peggy Ashcroft, Peter

Brook and Trevor Nunn, who becomes Director
Emeritus.

1990   The Other Place closes for rebuilding.

1991   Adrian Noble appointed Artistic Director. Artistic
advisors John Barton, Peter Brook. Terry Hands
and Trevor Nunn are also directors emeritus.

1995   David Brierley appointed a director emeritus

The Plays: 1948 Season

The Tragedy of Hamlet

HAMLET	Paul Scofield
THE GHOST	Esmond Knight
CLAUDIUS	Anthony Quayle
GERTRUDE	Diana Wynyard
POLONIUS	John Kidd
OPHELIA	Claire Bloom
LAERTES	William Squire

Produced by Michael Benthall
Scenery and Costumes by James Bailey
Incidental Music by Brian Easdale

The Taming of the Shrew

SLY	Esmond Knight
KATHARINA	Diana Wynyard

BIANCA	Mairhi Russell
PETRUCHIO	Anthony Quayle

Produced by Michael Benthall
Scenery and Costumes by Rosemary Vercoe
Incidental Music by Ernest Irving

Troilus and Cressida

PRIAM	Julian Amyes
HECTOR	Anthony Quayle
TROILUS	Paul Scofield
AENEAS	Manfred Priestley
PANDARUS	Noel Willman
CRESSIDA	Heather Stannard
AGAMEMNON	Michael Gwyn
ULYSSES	William Squire
PATROCLUS	Edmund Purdom
THERSITES	Esmond Knight
HELEN	Diana Wynyard

Produced by Anthony Quayle
Scenery and costumes by Motley
Incidental Music by Leslie Bridgewater

The Life and Death of King John

KING JOHN	Robert Helpmann
BLANCH	Claire Bloom
PHILIP OF FRANCE	Paul Scofield
CONSTANCE	Ena Burrill

| ARTHUR | Timothy Harley |
| PRINCE HENRY | Clifford Williams |

Produced by Michael Benthall
Scenery and costumes by Audrey Cruddas
Incidental music by Leslie Bridgewater

The Winter's Tale

LEONTES	Esmond Knight
HERMIONE	Diana Wynyard
MAMILIUS	Timothy Harley
ANTIGONUS	Michael Godfrey
PAULINA	Ena Burrill
CLOWN	Paul Scofield
TIME	William Squire
AUTOLYCUS	Alfie Bass
FLORIZEL	John Justin
PERDITA	Claire Bloom

Produced by Anthony Quayle
Scenery and Costumes by Motley
Incidental Music by Leslie Bridgewater

The Summer School

The first Summer School was held fifty years ago, from 23–30 August 1948, at Mason Croft, once the home of the novelist Marie Corelli and then The British Council Centre in Stratford (later to become The Shakespeare Institute of The University of Birmingham). It is interesting to see how little the general arrangement of The Summer School has changed in half a century. Though for some years it moved to the old Conference Hall of the theatre (now The Swan), it came back to Mason Croft in 1971 when Stanley Wells succeeded John Wilders as Director. It still takes place in August, still lasts just over a week and there are still two lectures each morning and visits to the plays in the afternoons and evenings, as well as social events. Over the years, however, the balance of speakers has shifted to include much greater participation by members of the theatre company.

The Summer School, or Course of Studies as it was more formally known in the first year was from the beginning under the auspices of the Governors of the Shakespeare Memorial

Theatre, now the RSC. In 1948 the programme was entitled *Shakespeare in Schools: A Course for Teachers of English.* Its Director was John Garrett, then Headmaster of Bristol Grammar School and part of his Foreword to the Programme reads:

The Course of Studies is intended primarily for teachers of English in British Schools. Teachers of English from Overseas will also be welcomed and the lectures will be opened to the general public as far as space permits.

The lectures have a two-fold purpose – to serve as a refresher course for teachers whose job it is to try to introduce Shakespeare to young people, and to make available to them some of the fruits of contemporary scholarship in their particular field; and to discuss the problems of the practical presentation of the plays in and beyond the classroom. It is often said that an adult interest in Shakespeare is lacking because his work has been murdered by classroom dissection. Though this is a doubtful half-truth, many schools have still to discover how to rally the enthusiasm of young people for the poet-dramatist who is their country's proudest possession. The course will attempt to explore some of these problems. By a close correlation of some of the lectures with visits to the Shakespeare Memorial Theatre particular importance will be placed on the ways and means by which it is possible to inculcate powers of discernment and a set of critical values to young people.

The Programme

AUGUST 23–30 1948

Monday 23 August

4.00 p.m.   Tea at The British Council Centre, Mason Croft

Reception and speeches of welcome by the Mayor of Stratford on Avon, Lt. Col. Fordham Flower OBE and the British Council representative for the Midlands Mr Ernest W. Burbidge, OBE

Tuesday 24 August

10.00 a.m.   F. I. VENABLES
Shakespeare in the School Curriculum

11.30 a.m.   JOHN GARRETT
Shakespeare's Conception of Comedy

Wednesday 25 August

10.00 a.m.   MRS BERYL BRAGG
Shakespeare on the School Stage

11.30 a.m.   I. A. SHAPIRO
Shakespeare's Conception of Tragedy

Thursday 26 August

10.00 a.m.   A. P. ROSSITER
             Shakespeare's English Chronicle and History
             Plays

11.30 a.m.   L. A. G. STRONG
             The Play of the Evening.

5.00 p.m.   Questions and Discussion

Friday 27 August

10.00 a.m.   MARGARET RAWLINGS
             Intonation: The Sound of Shakespeare

11.30 a.m.   FRANK BEECROFT AND CECIL DAY DEWIS
             Shakespeare's Use of Song

Saturday 28 August

10.00 a.m.   RONALD WATKINS
             Shakespeare as Poetic Dramatist

11.30.a.m.   NORMAN MARSHALL
             The Play of the Evening

Sunday 29 August

There will be Services at Holy Trinity Church at 8.00 a.m.
11.00 a.m. and 6.30 p.m. The Vicar, Canon Noel Prentice, will
welcome Members of the Course at all Services and make
reference to the teachers at the 11 o'clock Service.

3.30 p.m.   Tour of the Shakespeare Memorial Theatre

4.00 p.m.   Tea at the Shakespeare Memorial Theatre

5.30 p.m.   Discussion at the British Council Centre, Mason
            Croft

Monday 30 August

10.00 a.m.   MAURICE PERCEVAL
             The Mechanics of Elizabethan Production

11.30 a.m.   ERNEST BURBRIDGE
             A Laboratory Theatre for Schools

THE CONTRIBUTORS

ADRIAN NOBLE Born in Chichester in 1950. Artistic Director of the Royal Shakespeare Company since 1991

JANE LAPOTAIRE Born in 1944. Her roles with the RSC include Rosalind in *Love's Labour's Lost*, Gertrude in *Hamlet* and Queen Katharine in *Henry VIII*

RICHARD PASCO, CBE Born in 1926. His roles with the RSC include alternating Richard II and Bolingbroke with Ian Richardson in *Richard II*, Jacques in *As You Like It* and the title role in *Timon of Athens*

PHILIP VOSS His roles with the RSC include Menenius in *Coriolanus*, Quince in *A Midsummer Night's Dream* and Ulysses in *Troilus and Cressida*.

KENNETH BRANAGH Born in 1960. Has appeared in *Henry V* and *Hamlet* with the RSC, and also directed and starred in films of *Much Ado About Nothing* and *Hamlet*.

MICHAEL BILLINGTON Born in 1939 in Leamington Spa and educated at Warwick School. Theatre critic of *The Guardian* newspaper since 1971. He has written a number of books including biographies of Dame Peggy Ashcroft and, most recently, Harold Pinter.

LORNA FLINT Since her retirement as Head of English at Wycombe Abbey School, Lorna Flint has completed a Ph.D. degree at The Shakespeare Institute of the University of Birmingham in Stratford. She has attended every Summer School.

MARGARET YORKE Born in 1924. The author of a large number of best-selling crime novels, the latest of which is *Act of Violence* (Little Brown, 1997), and including several with a theatrical setting. A new novel will be published in 1998. Lists 'Theatre' as her principal hobby in *Who's Who*.

ANTONY SHER Born in South Africa in 1949. An Associate artist of the RSC since 1982. His roles with the company include the title role in *Richard III*, Malvolio in *Twelfth Night* and Shylock in *The Merchant of Venice* together with the title role in Marlowe's *Tamburlaine the Great* at The Swan. Antony Sher is also the author of the novels, *The Indoor Boy* and *Cheap Lives* and most recently of *Woza, Shakespeare*, about his performance as Titus Andronicus in South Africa

CICELY BERRY, OBE Born in 1926. The Voice Director of The RSC since 1969. Author of three books on voice training and voice production in the theatre.

DAVID BRIERLEY, OBE Began his career with the RSC in 1961. General Manager between 1968 and his retirement in 1996. He now lives in Cornwall.

ROGER HOWELLS Production Manager with the RSC, working in both the main house and The Swan, until his retirement in 1994.

TREVOR NUNN Born in 1940 in Suffolk. Artistic Director of the RSC 1968-87. Director Emeritus since 1986. Suceeded Sir Richard Eyre as Director of the National Theatre in 1997

GUY WOOLFENDEN Born in 1937. Composer in Residence with the RSC since 1963. He has composed incidental music for every one of Shakespeare's plays.

SIR DONALD SINDEN, CBE Born in 1923. First appeared at Stratford with the Shakespeare Memorial Company in 1946. Since then his roles with the RSC have included Plantagenet in *The Wars of the Roses*, Malvolio in *Twelfth Night*, Benedick in *Much Ado About Nothing* and the title roles in *Othello* and *King Lear*.

STANLEY WELLS Director of the RSC Summer School since 1971. Director of The Shakespeare Institute in Stratford and

Professor of Shakespeare Studies in the University of Birmingham 1988-97. Vice-Chairman of the Governors of the RSC. General Editor of The Oxford Shakespeare and author of a number of books on Shakespeare, mostly recently *Shakespeare: The Poet and his Plays* (Methuen 1997)